You Wrecked Me
You Complicate Me Duet Book 2

Isabel Jordan

Cover art: Dar Albert, Wicked Smart Designs

Cover photo: Lindee Robinson

Cover models: Shannon Lorraine and Anthony Parker

ISBN: 9781097734740

DEDICATION

This one's for all the readers who took a chance on a paranormal romance author's first contemporary rom com and liked it. Your support means the world to me!

ACKNOWLEDGMENTS

I always end up saying the same things over and over again in this section. So, this time, I'm just going to say a great big thank you to everyone who helped me get through the writing process for this book. Y'all know who you are. Hopefully I've done a good job of letting you know every day how important you are to me. But if I haven't, smack me upside the head, will you? Love you all!!

CHAPTER ONE

Sadie O'Connor always knew she'd see Gage Montgomery again one day.

She assumed it'd be at a family event. Her brother, Nick, was married to Gage's cousin, Grace, after all. And even though she'd successfully managed to avoid every Christmas, Thanksgiving, and birthday gathering for the past five years—thank you, *Luxe Adventures* magazine for all the travel assignments!—she always knew her luck would eventually run out.

She just never thought it would run out in a tiny hospital in middle-of-nowhere Montana...while she had a giant gash across her left butt cheek.

Sadie could blame her job for her current predicament, too. As author of the "Scaredy-Cat Travels" monthly column in *Luxe*, it was her job to go wherever the reader challenges came from, tackle said challenges, and report on them to let other scaredy- cat travelers know if they could handle the adventure.

To date, she'd been challenged to do everything from cliff diving in Acapulco, to ice climbing in Canmore, and white water rafting in British Columbia. Amazingly, she'd never been injured badly enough to require a hospital run.

Until today.

Who knew it'd be fly fishing in Montana that felled her?

Technically, she supposed, the fly fishing hadn't been a problem. As she'd expected, it was relaxing compared to most of her assignments. It wasn't until she was done fishing that the trouble really started.

"Trouble," in this case, was the sad-eyed dog by the side of the road who'd somehow managed to get himself completely tangled up in a length of barbed wire cattle fencing.

Walter, the grizzled guide who was hauling her tired ass back to the motel after her fishing adventure, had told her that animals got caught in barbed wire all the time out here. He said he'd call his rancher friend to get the poor dog out of the barbed wire as soon as possible. But had she listened? *Nooooooo.* She'd been bound and determined to help that dog. And what had her burst of goodwill done for her? It'd landed her in the hospital with a gash across her left ass cheek.

"Do you know when your last tetanus shot was, hon?" the nurse asked, iPad in hand, ready to type in her answer.

Sadie caught her lower lip between her teeth. Her first instinct was to lie because she hated shots. Like, *really* hated shots. She hated shots with the kind of passionate loathing she usually reserved for country music and big hairy spiders. But ultimately, she knew she needed to suck it up and adult her way through this. She'd be damned if she was going to get freakin' lockjaw because she was too much of a wuss to get a simple shot.

"It's been at least ten years ago," she admitted.

"Okay. We'll get you a tetanus shot. Any chance you're

YOU WRECKED ME / Isabel Jordan

pregnant?"

The only sex partner she'd had in the last five years was a seven-speed vibrator she'd named Chris Hemsworth. "Um…no. No chance. None. At. All."

The nurse, who'd said her name was Adele and looked like she was at least a hundred years old, gave Sadie a sympathetic head tilt and a sad nod. "I lost my Stanley last year. I've been going through a bit of a dry spell myself, hon. I feel your pain."

Sadie blinked at her. The thought of Adele having sex with her husband, who was probably also a hundred years old, almost made her cringe. Then she felt like the biggest bitch in the world when the rest of the woman's words sunk in. "Oh, I'm sorry for your loss."

Adele shrugged. "It wasn't any loss at all. Bastard left me for some child bride over in Missoula. The little tart's only fifty-two, for God's sake. He should be ashamed of himself for robbing the cradle like that. Fucker."

Sadie had no idea what to say to any of that, so she kept her mouth shut.

"Go ahead and flip over," Adele told her. "The doc will be right in when he's done with the dog. He'll stitch you up and I'll be back after that to give you your tetanus shot."

Sadie did as she was told, cringing when cold air hit her bare ass. You'd think *someone* would invent a paper hospital gown that actually covered a person's ass. But even knowing it was futile, she still tried to tug the thing closed. "Okay, thank…wait, what? I thought Walter said he was calling the vet in to look at the dog."

The poor thing had been dirty, way too skinny looking, and so tangled up in the barbed wire that it wasn't even struggling to get free anymore. It had obviously just resigned itself to the fact that it was going to die. Most of its cuts had looked superficial to Sadie, but Walter had promised he'd get the poor thing to the vet to get checked out.

Then a horrible thought occurred to her. Was she about to have her ass stitched up by a *vet*?

"Oh, there's no way Doc Watson was going to make it here tonight," Adele said. "I talked to him on his way out of town. He's delivering a calf up in Jasper. He won't be home till sometime late tomorrow, probably. It's okay, though. I asked Doc Montgomery to look him over and take care of him while I took your history. He should be done soon. I'll go get him for you."

The name *Montgomery* set off three different alarm systems in Sadie's body: one in her head, one in her heart, and one that originated in a place no one other than Chris Hemsworth had been in a long, long time.

But there was no way it could be *him*, right? What would a hotshot surgeon like Gage Montgomery be doing in a tiny little town like Last Chance, Montana?

Montgomery was a common name, her brain told her while her heart panicked and her lady bits hoped and prayed it really *was* Gage about to walk through that door.

When this whole thing was over and she no longer had a giant gash on her ass, she was going to have a long, stern talk with her heart and lady bits. It had been five years. It was high time they stopped

8

overreacting at the mere mention of Gage Montgomery.

The fact of the matter was that she was a different person now. She wasn't the scared, pathetic little girl she'd been when he last saw her. The old Sadie would've fallen apart in his presence. But the new Sadie fell apart for no man. Why, if Gage walked through that door right now, she'd confidently look him dead in the eye and say...

"Sadie? Sadie *O'Connor*?"

Whatever she was going to confidently look him dead in the eye and say withered and died in her throat as she glanced over her shoulder—past her bare butt cheeks—and up into the face of the man she'd been ruthlessly *not* thinking about for the past five years.

God, he looked good. Downright lickable—all six feet and however many inches of him. It should be illegal to look like *that*. Why did anyone have to be *that* good looking? It was gratuitous, really.

His shocked expression shifted into something decidedly cockier and...smirkier, which made her wonder if she could actually *die* of embarrassment, right here in this hospital, with her ass in the air.

Or maybe she could dive out a window like Jason Bourne and make a run for it? Or pretend she was someone else? Her own evil twin, perhaps?

But since none of that seemed feasible, she squeezed her eyes shut, and asked, "I said that out loud, didn't I?"

"Oh, don't worry, hon," Adele said from somewhere behind Gage. "No harm in speaking the truth. Just don't grab his ass, m'kay? I had to have a stern talk with old lady Hendricks last week about personal space and sexual harassment, and I'd really hate to have to repeat that."

So this is what being so embarrassed you wish the floor would swallow you up feels like. Huh. You learn something new every day.

She'd gone five years without seeing or hearing anything about Gage Montgomery. And now, in the middle of Bumfuck Nowhere, here she was, bare ass in the air, right in front of the smirky, incredible looking jerk.

You'd think that a woman who made her living writing would be able to come up with a pithy quote from a literary genius that would apply to the situation and make her sound smart and witty and coy all at the same time. But sadly, the only thing Sadie came up with was a Bobby Singer quote from *Supernatural.*

"Balls."

CHAPTER TWO

"You're gonna *love* the surprise I have for you behind curtain one. This is super exciting."

Gage Montgomery had repressed a sigh at Adele's comment. First of all, the Clinton Hitchcock Memorial Hospital ER in Last Chance, Montana, only *had* one curtain. There was one exam room with an actual door, and one curtained-off area where an overflow patient could be seen.

And yes, that was "patient," singular, because there were never more than two patients at once in this hole-in-the-wall ER. But still, Adele insisted on referring to the ER as "The Pit" and their single curtained area as "curtain one" like they were on fucking *Grey's Anatomy* or something.

Second of all, nothing *super exciting* ever happened here. The wildest things that ever passed through those ER doors were the Dorsey twins, toddler boys who were fond of shoving objects up each other's noses, and Leo, the rodeo clown who got drunk and fell off his barstool at the Copper Still every Friday night like clockwork.

And finally, he never really *loved* any of Adele's surprises. Her first surprise of the night had been putting a dog in his exam room and making him clean and stitch the thing up. An hour, three phone calls to the local vet who was out of town, and lots and lots of cursing later, the dog was happily napping on his hospital bed in the exam room like he belonged there.

But when Gage pulled back the curtain and saw an injured ass, he thought maybe he owed Adele an apology. At least he wouldn't be pulling M&Ms out of a Dorsey's nose or checking Leo for signs of a concussion. There was probably, at the very least, a good story attached to this ass.

Then he'd glanced at her chart, and her name jumped off it and punched him in the gut.

"Sadie? Sadie O'Connor?" he'd muttered in shock.

She'd blushed—he'd never seen a woman's *entire* body turn red when she blushed—and muttered how lickable he looked, followed by something about balls, and his shock was replaced by amusement. Mostly.

If he was being honest with himself—which he almost never was because, fuck, that was *exhausting* when you had as many issues as Gage had—he'd admit that what he was feeling now was a creamy blend of shock, amusement, lust, and anger.

The shock was understandable. He was in the middle of nowhere, face-to-face—well, face-to-*ass*, he supposed—with a woman who'd actively avoided him for years. She was like a wraith—nothing but a beautiful memory who'd vanished into thin air. Even her brother and Gage's cousin, Grace, refused to discuss Sadie whenever Gage was around. So, to say that seeing her *here*, now, was a surprise, was a huge understatement. Like saying the ocean is a tad damp, or that DC superhero movies only sucked a little ass.

(DC superhero movies sucked A LOT of ass...just to be perfectly clear.)

The amusement he was feeling was pretty understandable, too. The woman who'd actively avoided him for five years was on his exam table with her injured ass in the air, and she'd just told him he was lickable without realizing she'd said it out loud. Who wouldn't be amused by that? It was like a gift from Karma herself.

The lust? Also understandable. Five years ago, Sadie had been the most beautiful woman he'd ever laid eyes on. Now? She'd somehow managed to age into a woman even *more* beautiful than the one who'd knocked him on his ass back then.

But it wasn't just the big navy-blue eyes, flawless olive complexion, pouty Angelina Jolie mouth, or the thick dark hair he just wanted to wrap his fist around that drew him in. There was something in her eyes that hadn't been there five years ago—a strength and confidence that was sexy as hell.

And then there was that ass to consider...

Even with a gash on one cheek, it was obvious that her ass was even better than it had been when they first met. If he hadn't missed his guess, Sadie had put on some weight since he'd last seen her, and it had apparently gone to *all* the right places.

The anger he was feeling? Well...that was a little more complicated.

Even though they'd had the opposite of a meet-cute—she'd been on the verge of marrying his cousin, Michael, after all—Gage thought they'd shared…something.

When Sadie got food poisoning at one of the pre-wedding dinners, Gage had been the one to take care of her, since Michael had a tendency to gag at the mere *thought* of vomit, blood, or phlegm. They'd gotten to know each other fairly well during the three days they were stuck together in her sick room and had developed somewhat of a bond over their similarly shitty upbringings, love of '80s movies, and nerd tendencies they weren't willing to discuss with anyone else. (Yes, they'd both been huge D&D fans in high school. What of it?)

They'd also had an immediate, absolutely smokin' physical chemistry that had confused and thrilled the hell out of Gage in equal measure.

Or at least he *thought* they'd had all that. How could he know for sure after she pulled her *Runaway Bride* routine and left Michael—and Gage—in the dust without so much as a goodbye?

"It's been a while, Sadie," he finally said.

"Wait…you know her, Dr. Montgomery?" Adele asked, her gaze bobbing between Sadie and Gage.

"I thought I did, but that was a long time ago," he muttered, more to himself than to Adele.

Oh, but Sadie heard him. And the glare she leveled him with was sharp enough to slice the skin right off his bones.

Huh. That was new. The Sadie he'd known had been sweet and slow to anger. He'd really liked that Sadie. But this new Sadie who was shooting fire from her eyes? She was crazy sexy.

He shook his head. Damn, he really needed to get some sleep.

His judgement must be impaired by exhaustion. Why else would he find a woman hitting him with *fuck off* eyes hot?

"Thanks, Adele," he said to his nurse, putting as much *you can go now* into his tone as possible.

Adele raised a brow at him, offering up her own *fuck off* expression at being dismissed before she got any good gossip. But thankfully, she didn't argue and closed the privacy curtain around them before flouncing back out to the admissions desk as fast as her squeaky-soled Nikes would carry her.

"So," he began casually, snapping on a set of surgical gloves, "I take it this injury has something to do with the dog I stitched up?"

Sadie groaned and dropped her forehead into her palm. "Tell me this is a joke," she muttered. "You can't be the doctor."

"Johns Hopkins would disagree."

"I mean, I'm in the middle of nowhere," she went on. "You're from New York. How are you even here right now?"

He leaned against the wall and crossed his arms over his chest. "Medical school is expensive. Sometimes hospitals make deals with students offering to pay for their schooling in exchange for a certain number of years of service following their residency."

To Gage, it was a no-brainer. Work at Clinton Hitchcock (where no doctor had ever stayed for more than a few weeks, apparently, and the administration was desperate to hire anyone who knew how to wield a scalpel) for five years in exchange for them paying back all his school loans? Hell, yeah. It'd take him decades to pay those loans back otherwise, and he didn't have any desire to be poor for that long.

Besides, his time with Clinton was almost done and he'd be free to go wherever he wanted to practice. It'd all been worth it. He glanced back down at Sadie's ass, which she was surreptitiously trying to cover by futilely tugging at the corners of her hospital gown.

His time here was *especially* worth it *today*.

"You can't be my doctor," she said again. "I need another doctor. *Any* other doctor would be fine."

He frowned. Well, that was a little insulting. He'd trained under the best at Hopkins and turned out to be a damn fine general surgeon. He'd done every appendectomy, gall bladder removal, and colectomy the good folks of Last Chance had needed for the past five years. He was certainly capable of placing a few stitches in her ass cheek. He knew how to do it without leaving so much as a hint of a scar, for God's sake. And she was ready to cast him aside for any other doctor who just happened to be in the vicinity tonight?

"Sorry to disappoint," he said dryly, "but it's just me here at the moment. The relief doc won't be in for another two hours." Not to mention the relief doctor was roughly 120 years old and had narcolepsy. Gage had once found him face-down in a bowl of tapioca in the cafeteria. "If you want that taken care of so you can be on your way, you're stuck with me."

He could see the struggle on her face. She was debating if her injury was worse than her potential embarrassment. She must have decided it was, because she let out a resigned sigh and quit trying to pull her gown closed over her ass.

Gage desperately wanted to make an inappropriate joke about how she was showing him her ass and he didn't even have to buy her dinner first. He'd never even *consider* saying such a thing to any other patient. But with Sadie…he was morbidly curious to see what it took to make her do that whole-body blush again.

But he held back, deciding she'd probably hop off the table and leave if he pushed his luck.

"All right then," he said. "Let's get started."

CHAPTER THREE

"This is cold and will probably sting a little," he murmured. "Sorry."

Sadie inhaled sharply. Not because of the alcohol wipe he'd just swiped over her gash—even though it had, as Gage had warned, felt like a blast of freakin' Arctic air across her skin and stung like a bitch—but because he'd put his other hand on her ass as he examined the area.

She could feel the heat of his skin through his glove and his hand was large enough that it covered a huge portion of her ass. And her ass wasn't exactly small these days.

But what really sucked? She *liked* how his hand on her ass felt. She hadn't had so much as a twinge of attraction to anyone she'd met in the past five years, hadn't had a hand on her body other than her own in that time, and she'd never really missed it.

Until now. Until *him.*

Her body had practically been a block of ice for five years and it decided to thaw out *now.*

She'd had no business being attracted to him five years ago and she had no business being attracted to him now, but…yeah. Here they were, with his hand on her ass and her lady bits tingling in a way they hadn't tingled in *way* too long.

"So tell me how this happened," he said.

Thankful for something—anything—that might distract her from her tingling lady bits and his big, warm hand on her ass, she launched into the story of how she'd been on her way home from her fly-fishing assignment when she'd seen the poor dog, trapped in barbed wire on the outer reaches of a cattle ranch.

With Walter's help, she'd gotten the dog untangled, but she'd managed to lose her footing and landed ass-first in the barbed wire herself.

"Well," Gage said when she finished her story, "you'll be happy to know the dog is perfectly fine. He's had a bath, only had a few cuts that needed stitching up, and is currently sleeping in our only real exam room. He snores, by the way. Loudly."

In that case, all her embarrassment and pain was well worth it. "Was Walter able to find the dog's owners?"

"Walter said he wouldn't know where to start. He's never seen a dog like that in town, and he knows everyone. The dog looked like a stray to me. I don't know what he *should* weigh, but he looks way too skinny to me, too. And he about took my hand off when I gave him my dinner, so I'd say it's been a while since he's eaten."

And that's when Sadie's heart started getting warmer than her lady bits. It was something she'd noticed about Gage when she first met him—on the surface, he was a grumpy, antisocial jerk. But when you got to know him, you saw that he really was a good, decent guy. The kind of guy who'd give a stray dog his dinner.

19

"Thank you for taking care of him," she said, her throat tight with an annoying lump of emotion that had lodged there.

In typical Gage-fashion, he shrugged off her thanks with a noncommittal grunt, completely unwilling to acknowledge he was a nice guy. While she might have changed a lot since they'd last seen each other, it appeared he hadn't changed at all.

Sadly, that included his looks. The grumpy bastard was every bit as sexy now as he had been five years ago. Was it too much to ask that he be balding and paunchy with bad teeth or something?

But *noooooooo*, not Gage Montgomery. His thick dark hair was as lush and unruly as ever, and it practically begged her fingers to tangle in it. Was it as soft as it looked?

He still looked like he spent every second outside of work exercising, if the biceps visibly testing the strength of his lab coat's sleeves were any indication. And his eyes…

Those light, greenish-blue eyes of his were every bit as hot and intense and…hungry-looking as they'd been five years ago. And it still took little more than a glance in her direction from those eyes to turn her knees to pudding.

So even though Sadie had done a good bit of growing up since she'd last seen Gage, she apparently wasn't ready to adult all on her own just yet. Because surely good…adulting didn't include falling apart just because a man was gorgeous, smelled better than anything she'd ever smelled, and looked at her like she was the last Reese's cup in the package.

"The vet will be back tomorrow," Gage said. "He said you

could bring the dog by anytime and he'd check and make sure I hadn't done anything that'll eventually kill it. His confidence in my abilities was *super* flattering."

She could bring the dog by anytime. Keeping the dog wasn't something Sadie considered when she decided to help it. She imagined few people who jumped in to rescue dogs thought about what they'd do if no one else came forward to claim the animal.

"I'm assuming Last Chance doesn't have a dog rescue or animal shelter," she murmured.

He snorted. "Well, you've been to the hospital, and I assume you're staying at the motel. If you've also been to the gas station, the grocery store, the bar, and the diner, you've seen everything there is to see in Last Chance. Anything else is at least 50 miles away."

In that case, Sadie supposed she'd just adopted a dog. It's not like she could just turn it loose to fend for itself after all it had been through. "Guess I'll take it with me when I go back to motel."

"There," he said, and she heard the snap of his gloves as he removed them. "This wasn't as bad as it initially looked. I cleaned it up and was able to use liquid sutures instead of sewing it up. It'll probably sting tonight, but in a day or so it won't even hurt at all. I am going to prescribe an oral antibiotic for you to stave off any infection, but that's really just me being super cautious."

"That's great. Thank you."

As he typed some notes in her chart, Sadie rolled to her side and pulled her hospital gown closed over her butt. "Can I leave now?" she asked.

He glanced up from his charting and pinned with her a look so potent she had to force herself not to break eye contact. She knew that look. He wanted to say something, but thought better of it. She could only imagine all the things he might want to say to her after all these years.

And she'd be willing to bet that 90% of those things wouldn't be complimentary.

Not that she blamed him. She had run away from him as far and as fast as she could go in her fancy wedding shoes—and she'd been running ever since. Never staying in any one place longer than it took to complete a new assignment for *Lux*. And it'd been good for her, too. Until lately, of course.

Lately she'd found herself getting tired. Tired of the travel. Tired of being away from her brother, who was her only real family. Tired of motel rooms and fast food. The idea of settling down, maybe buying a house and working from home instead of traveling all the time was suddenly way more appealing than it had ever been before.

And now she had a dog to think about…

Maybe this dog was a sign of some kind. A sign that it was indeed time to settle down. Start writing the book she'd been mulling over for the past few months.

Was seeing Gage again a sign, too? Maybe she was supposed to make amends before moving on with her new, settled-down, dog-having life? She supposed she did owe him an explanation. He had been a big part of her decision to call off her wedding, after all. He probably deserved to know the whole story.

She swallowed hard. "Um, Gage, about the night of my wedding, I wanted to tell you—"

He slammed the iPad down on the bedside table so hard she flinched. "Don't. I get it. You were just the girl my cousin was going to marry. Your leaving wasn't any of my business."

Except that it *was*, an oft-ignored little voice inside her heart whispered. It *was* his business. It was ultimately her crazy, messed-up feelings for Gage that made her realize she couldn't marry Michael.

And those feelings hadn't been one-sided. She was sure of it. There'd been that one night when he'd helped her recover from food poisoning (and yes, it was just as romantic as it sounded, which was not at all. Not in any way. No. Romance. Whatsoever.) that they'd shared...something. Nothing physical, of course, because she wasn't a cheater and Gage would never do that to Michael. But still, their...whatever it was hadn't all been her imagination.

Had it?

She cleared her throat. "It *was* your business. I owed you, at the very least, a goodbye. We were...friends."

Oh, God, why had she said that? They hadn't been friends! She'd daydreamed about biting his lower lip, for God's sake. You can't be friends with someone after daydreaming about biting their lower lip while they were eating a club sandwich across the table from you and your fiancé. "I'm sorry," she added quietly.

His gaze narrowed on her. Not in a mean way, but like he was curious. He was studying her like a bug pinned to a board in science class.

She probably would've preferred a mean look, actually. This look was just unnerving.

After a long, awkward, loaded silence, he said, "Adele will be in to give you your tetanus shot, but you're all set. You can take the dog and go whenever you're ready. Goodbye, Sadie."

And with that, he turned and stalked away from her as if the finality of his goodbye hadn't just hit her like a gunshot to the chest.

Well, she thought, so much for *signs* and making amends.

CHAPTER FOUR

Gage waited impatiently, silently stewing, until Grace answered her phone. Before she could say anything, he barked, "Did you know?"

"That you're a rude asshole who doesn't understand proper phone etiquette?" she shot back without hesitation. "Yes. I knew that. *Hello*, by the way, you douchebag."

He pinched the bridge of his nose and sighed. He supposed he'd walked right into that one and probably deserved it. Not that he'd ever admit that to her. "Did you know that Sadie was coming to Last Chance?"

There was a loaded pause, and Gage imagined Grace was taking a moment to choose her words carefully. Lawyers had a tendency to do that. But eventually, she said, "I did."

"And you didn't think that was worth mentioning to me?"

"Not really. I mean, I assumed she'd be in town, socializing with people, and you'd be holed up in your cabin like a creepy extra from *Deliverance*. I figured you'd never even see her, frankly."

He took exception to the *Deliverance* thing. Gage was antisocial, sure, but not *creepy*. So he preferred to be alone. What was wrong with that? "You should have told me," he muttered.

She sighed. "You're right. I should have. I'm sorry. I just

thought that if you knew she was in town, you'd go out of your way to avoid her. And if you happened to run into her by accident, well…maybe it wouldn't be such a bad thing."

Grace was now happily married and almost nine months pregnant. So because she was coupled-up, settled and happy, she wanted *everyone* to be coupled-up, settled and happy.

It probably didn't ever occur to her that some people just weren't cut out for the coupled-up, settled and happy lifestyle. Gage was a prime example of that.

"I'd say running into me didn't exactly make her day either," Gage said, then filled Grace in on what had happened.

"Oh, my God," Grace said when Gage finished his story. "I don't know whether that's all really hilarious, or really sad. You just walked away from her?"

"Walking away from each other seems to be our thing."

He sounded like a petulant child even to his own ears, and he didn't care for it. Not one bit.

"You know, most couples have a song or a funny little inside joke they share. Walking away is a terrible thing for a couple to have."

"Which is fine, because we're not a couple," he reminded her.

"You're at least going to help her get back to her motel, aren't you?" Grace asked. "I've been to Last Chance, remember? I know there aren't any Ubers."

Gage rubbed a hand over the back of his neck. "I'm sure Adele can help her make some kind of arrangement."

Grace didn't say anything for a moment, and Gage could

practically hear the storm gathering on her end of the line. She wasn't one to keep her thoughts to herself *before* she got pregnant. Now? Pregnancy hormones had pretty much demolished whatever filter had ever existed between Grace's brain and mouth. He braced himself for what was to come.

He didn't have to wait long.

"You know," she began, her tone short and staccato and sharp enough to split a hair, "I always stood up for you. Anytime you ever did anything bad when we were kids—I stood up for you. Told everyone what a good guy you were, even when you did your damn-level best to convince us all you weren't."

Gage knew she was right. She'd always been his advocate, even when he didn't think he deserved one. In his mind, he'd just been the trailer-trash cousin who had to move into the bedroom next to hers when they were kids because his parents never came home after a drug run. It'd been hard to accept that he was worthy of love and respect from someone like Grace and her family, even though they were technically his family, too.

And if anyone thought he was a dick now? Well, they hadn't seen *anything* like what'd he'd done when he was a kid. He'd picked fights, shoplifted, drank, smoked, broke curfew, failed classes—you name the stereotypical "bad seed" behavior and he'd done it.

Sarah and David—Grace's parents—had sent him to a therapist when he was a teenager. It was that therapist who helped Gage realize he was acting out in response to finally being in a home where everyone loved each other. He wasn't sure how to accept love, so he did his best to push them all away—to reject them before they could reject him. Because rejection? Now *that* was something he understood.

But Grace never gave up on him. She patiently tolerated his shitty behavior until he grew out of all his anger issues.

Well, he grew out of *most* of his anger issues, he should say.

Gage sighed. "Grace, I know you were always—"

"And in all honesty," she went on as if he hadn't spoken, "Nick wasn't too happy with you after Sadie's near-miss wedding. He couldn't blame his sister, obviously, so he blamed you. And do you know who stood up for you?"

"I'm guessing it was you," he murmured, even though he was sure she wasn't actually expecting him to speak yet.

"It was me, Gage. It's always *me*. So when you tell me you plan to leave an injured woman in the middle of nowhere to fend for herself where anything could happen to her—"

"Jesus, it's not like we're in Beirut or something. There hasn't been a real crime in Last Chance since 1954, for God's—"

"—then I have no idea how I'm going to defend you this time. And frankly, I'm not even sure I want to."

He was about to defend *himself* when he heard the sniffling on Grace's end. "Oh, for the love of God," he muttered. "Are you crying again?"

This was another delightful symptom of Grace's pregnancy. His normally level-headed cousin was awash with hormones that made her cry for no reason and without notice. And once the tears started,

Gage knew he was done for. He had no defenses in place to deal with a crying woman. He found that he'd pretty much do anything to make the tears stop.

Another sniffle, then a watery, "No. It's fine. Just do whatever you think is right. I'm sure it'll all work out fine in the end. I'm sure Sadie won't be picked up by a serial killer while she's hitchhiking back to her motel. I'm sure I won't have to tell Nick that his *baby* sister *died* because you were too much a whiny, pansy-assed *tool* to offer her some common courtesy. And even though the doctor says my blood pressure is too high, and that I should avoid stress as much as possible, I'll do my best not to worry about my injured sister-in-law, who may or may not end up dead in a ditch in Last Chance…"

"I'll pay you a thousand dollars to stop," he begged. "Just…stop. I'll drive her back to her motel. Will that make it stop?"

She sniffled again. "Yes. And you can keep your thousand and use it to come see me when the baby's born."

"Fine," he said through gritted teeth.

"And will you at least *try* to be nice to her?"

"Don't push your luck."

CHAPTER FIVE

Sadie would've bet every dollar she had on her—which was only about eight since she hadn't yet found an ATM in Last Chance—that it hadn't been Gage's idea to help her.

He'd barely said a word since he'd told her back at the hospital that he was driving her back to the motel.

Didn't *ask* her if she *wanted* a ride back to the motel, mind you. *Told* her he was driving her.

By this point, Sadie was in a pretty foul mood and would've told him to eat a dick if she'd had a better way of getting back to town on her own. But since her only other options were to stay at the hospital until Adele's shift ended the next morning and ride with her, or walk the five miles between the hospital and motel, fireman-carrying an injured dog who looked really skinny but was still big enough to be heavy, Sadie decided she should just keep her sass to herself and accept the ride.

Well, even if her driver was less than cordial, at least she was riding in comfort, she thought, leaning her head back against the buttery-soft, heated leather seats of Gage's ginormous luxury SUV.

Sadie squealed when the dog leaned forward from his position in the back seat and swiped his tongue up the side of her face, chin to eyebrow. She glanced over her shoulder and met the big, warm brown eyes of her new dog, who was practically vibrating with excitement, the tip of his tail swishing enthusiastically on the seat.

"Well, hello there, baby," she cooed. "Are you feeling better?" The tail swished faster and she laughed. "I'll take that as a yes."

"I'm going to take it as a he-can-walk-his-own-heavy-ass-around-from-now-on," Gage grumbled. "I wasn't looking forward to carrying him again."

Sadie's adrenaline had been pumping so hard when she pulled the dog free of the barbed wire that she hadn't even really noticed how big he was. Even malnourished, she guessed he had to weigh at least a hundred pounds. To get him into Walter's truck she'd had to lift his hind end while Walter lifted his upper half.

Gage, of course, showoff that he was, had hefted the dog up into his arms like he weighed no more than a Chihuahua. *Stupid, antisocial, muscle-y jerk.*

She turned back to the dog. "Well, I suppose I need to name you, don't I, baby?"

More tail swishing.

"Hmmm..." she said, mostly just thinking out loud, "wonder what kind of dog you are."

"I'm still not sure it's a dog," Gage said. "His feet are the size of dinner plates and he weighs more than you do."

"Adele didn't take my weight, so you have no idea how much I weigh," she scoffed.

He glanced over at her and flicked his eyes over her body in a way that said, *yes, I know exactly what you weigh and exactly what you'd look like naked.*

And there were the full-body tingles again. Damn it! How did he *do* that?

Gage shifted his tingle-inducing gaze back to the road and said, "I sent the vet a picture. He said this guy is probably some kind of Irish Wolfhound/Great Dane mix."

Sadie turned in her seat and scratched behind the dog's ear. He leaned his giant head into her hand and huffed out a satisfied breath. "Well, in that case, I'm calling you Colin Farrell."

Gage snorted. "Why Colin Farrell?"

"Because he's handsome and Irish, obviously."

"Oh, obviously."

His tone was desert-dry, so the only thing letting Sadie know he was mildly amused was the slight upward curve of one side of his mouth. That was pretty much the entire extent of Gage Montgomery's emotional repertoire: annoyed, angry, intense, and mildly amused.

Except for that one night when he'd taken care of her. She'd seen a different side to him them. Especially when he...

Nope. Not going there. No good will come from living in that *place.*

And just as she knew it was useless to live in the past, Sadie knew ignoring this...*thing* she had with Gage was equally pointless. They needed to work out their differences, once and for all. If not for them, then for Grace and Nick. After all, it wasn't as if Sadie could avoid all family events until the end of time.

And since she knew Gage would never start the conversation,

she supposed she'd have to pull up her big-girl panties and do it herself.

"Gage," she began, silently cursing her voice for breaking like a pimply teenager about to ask a boy to the Sadie Hawkins dance, "I know you don't want to talk about this—or anything else, for that matter—but I really would like for you to give me a chance to explain what happened at the wedding."

A muscle in his jaw jumped and his eyes narrowed almost imperceptibly on the road ahead of them. "I was there," he bit out. "I know what happened."

Sadie felt the nervous wave of words rising, threatening to spill off her tongue at any moment. She knew if she opened her mouth, she was going to vomit words all over him. It was going to be humiliating, and he was going to think she was bat-shit crazy. And even knowing all that, she was powerless to stop herself from opening her mouth.

"Look, I was young and stupid and thought I knew what love was, but looking back at it now, I was never *really* in love with Michael. It was more that I admired him and was attracted to him and really wanted what he had, you know? That family—*your* family—that kind of…unconditional love. I'd never had that before, but I'd always craved it. I felt like I needed it, I guess, so I convinced myself I was in love with Michael and wanted to marry him. But when I saw what Grace and Nick had, I realized that was what love *really* looked like, and I was never going to have that with Michael. But I thought that I *could* someday have that with *you* because…" *Oh, God, please stop talking!* "…the first time I saw you it was like getting hit by lightning or something, which sounds trite, I realize…"

He side-eyed her like she was a bomb about to go off. Oh, why couldn't she stop talking?

"...but then I *talked* to you and you took care of me when I was sick and it was like..." *Just shoot me in the head. That's the only way this is going to stop. Only my bloody death will end it.* "...I felt a connection to you that I'd never felt before. And frankly that scared the crap out of me, so I ran away—from the wedding, from Michael, from you...from myself, really. It was all about me, and I'm so sorry that I made it all about me and didn't take everyone else's feelings into account and ruined...whatever we could've—"

Gage reached over and grabbed her hand, giving her fingers a firm squeeze. "Stop," he said quietly.

"Oh, thank you," she breathed out on a gusty sigh.

He shook his head. "Look, I get it, OK? You did what you needed to do for yourself and there's nothing wrong with that. You *should* be looking out for yourself. Sure, I would've liked a chance to say goodbye...or whatever. But you really *didn't* owe me anything. I don't have any right to be a dick to you. It's fine. We're fine."

The relief that washed over her was so overwhelming she was afraid she'd start blubbering if she said too much, so she just squeezed his hand and asked, "So, you forgive me? You don't hate me?"

"There's nothing to forgive. And of course I don't hate you. I never did." Under his breath, so quiet she almost didn't hear it, he added, "I never could."

All the tension she'd been carrying in her shoulders, jaw, and neck eased and she took a deep, relaxed breath for the first time since she'd seen Gage standing in that doorway, wearing his scrubs, looking grumpy and irritated and all kinds of hot. "Thank you," she whispered. "I can't tell you what that means to me."

He side-eyed her again, frowning a little. "You're not going to cry, are you? Because I take it all back if you're going to cry."

She barked out a laugh/snort combo that made her cringe before telling him, "No. I am most definitely *not* going to cry. I'm just relieved that we don't have to be awkward with each other anymore."

He smirked a little, reminding her that men who looked like him were *never* awkward. *Awkward* was for losers. Losers who spewed their innermost thoughts in bouts of verbal diarrhea so embarrassing they made you want to jump through closed hospital windows to escape the sound of your own voice.

Losers like her.

People who looked like Gage were way too cool for *awkward*. She kind of admired that about him, all while hating him for it.

"Can we be friends now that the weirdness is behind us?" she finally asked, totally proud of herself for not telling him what she was really thinking, which was that he smelled like heaven…if heaven had lots of warm, clean male skin. And testosterone.

Because she'd be willing to bet that pure, alpha-male testosterone smelled like Gage Montgomery. If she could package that smell, make it into dryer sheets or something, and sell it to horny women everywhere she'd be a freakin' *billionaire*.

He glanced over at her, his eyes dropping to her mouth for just a split second. It was such a quick glance that she probably wouldn't have even noticed it…except that when Gage looked at her like that it made her lips tingle. Her nipples, too. But that was another story entirely.

"Friends," he said, almost like it was a foreign word he intended to look up in a dictionary when he got home. "That'd be a first."

"You've never had women friends?"

"I can't remember the last time I had a friend. Woman *or* man. I'm guessing family doesn't count, right?"

She shifted in her seat to face him fully. "Gage Montgomery, you've been in Last Chance for five years. You haven't made any friends in that time? What do you do when you're not working?"

He shrugged. "I read. Watch TV. Work out. You know, usual stuff."

Sadie sputtered for a moment. "But, I've met *awesome* people in Last Chance and I've only been here a few *days*. How is it that you haven't made *any* friends in five years?"

He ran a hand through his hair, looking decidedly frustrated with the direction of their conversation. "In case you haven't noticed, I'm not exactly friendly. I don't really like people all that much, and they seem to return the sentiment." Another shrug. "I don't really have to be likeable to be good at my job, and I've never needed much of anything from people. I'm happy being alone most of the time. I never really thought it was a big deal."

And that's when Sadie remembered something Gage had told her when they were holed up in her sick room right before her ill-fated wedding.

My parents ran off when I was five. I learned pretty quickly that the only person I could always count on was myself.

Sadie understood. She'd been a founding member of the Pathetic Childhood Club herself. When they had the kind of upbringing Gage and Sadie had, children usually went in one of two directions: they became people-pleasers who did anything and everything to be as likeable and as un-ditchable as possible (*cough*Sadie*), or they became loners who never trusted anyone (*cough*Gage*).

Gage was too good a person to be alone. He was the kind of person who gave his dinner to a skinny dog, for God's sake. He deserved to have people in his life who knew what a good guy he was. The thought of him, so far away from his family, with no friends, no one to talk to about his day or have beers with on the weekend…well, it made her heart hurt in ways she'd rather not contemplate for too long.

Sadie cleared her throat to dislodge the uncomfortable lump of emotion that had settled there. "It is a big deal. I'll be your friend, and maybe having me as a friend will help you want to make more. It's not much, but it's something, at least. That'll be how I repay you for helping me tonight."

He gave her that tiny, barely there, smug, half-smile of his that somehow made her blood boil and her panties wet all at the same time. "Well, the hospital will be sending a bill, so you can probably just get away with repaying me the traditional way."

She scowled at him. "Now you're just being willfully obtuse. How can you expect to build a medical practice—here or anywhere else, for that matter—when you have the bedside manner of a rabid Rottweiler?"

He whistled. "Wow. Harsh."

And yet he didn't sound at all offended. "Seriously. You should make an effort to get to know more people. I guarantee that spending time with people is better than spending time alone."

"I don't know. I'm pretty fucking delightful to spend time with."

Her lip twitched, but she wouldn't give him the satisfaction of smiling. "Hear that a lot, do you?"

"I tell myself that every day. Sometimes twice a day."

She just kept her gaze on him until he relented with a chuckle. "Fine. We'll be friends."

Sadie fought the urge to fist-pump. If he let her into his life, Gage wouldn't become—or stay, she supposed—a grumpy recluse who only showed his face at the hospital.

She was so happily lost in her musings for the rest of the drive that it wasn't until Gage pulled up to her motel that she realized she'd been holding his hand for the past half-hour.

So much for not making things awkward between them.

CHAPTER SIX

Bedbugs. Fate—or Karma, maybe—was officially fucking with him via bedbugs.

When Gage had pulled up to the motel, he hadn't even noticed the unusual amount of activity out front. He'd been too distracted by the fact that Sadie was still holding his hand.

The feel of her silky skin and tiny, delicate-boned hand touching him, holding onto him like it was the most natural thing in the world, made it hard for him to breathe normally. It was almost as if he was afraid that if he so much as *breathed* wrong, she'd pull away.

So, barely breathing and clinging to her hand like it was a fucking lifeline, he failed to notice that the motel's guests—all three of them—were fleeing from the place like it was on fire.

A quick chat with the night manager revealed someone, a former guest, had called in a report of bedbugs in room 105. Everyone felt like the whole thing was a prank since the place was so clean you could eat off the floor. But just to be safe, it needed to be checked and possibly treated, and all guests needed to make other lodging arrangements for the next few days, maybe even longer.

Since there was only one place to rent a room in Last Chance, Gage made the only suggestion he could think of that would keep him from driving Sadie another fifty miles that night.

She could stay at his house.

Grace would laugh her *ass* off when she heard about this. Hell, for all he knew, it might've even been Grace who'd called in the bedbug threat, knowing it might throw him and Sadie together for a few more days. Under normal circumstances Grace was diabolical. But with pregnancy hormones surging through her veins?

Fucking. Scary.

"Can I help?"

Gage hefted Sadie's bag over one shoulder and lifted the giant, slobbering dog—Colin Farrell, he corrected with a mental eye roll—into his arms. Gage considered making the giant bastard walk in on his own, but was half afraid the damn thing would bust a stitch if he tried to move too fast. The last thing Gage needed was to get stuck with more emergency vet work.

"I've got it," he said, trying not to feel offended that she kept offering to help him carry stuff in. He was a piss poor excuse for a gentleman, but he wasn't so far gone that he expected her to carry in a bag that looked to weigh more than her and a dog the size of a pony. "I don't need any help."

Except, as he climbed the steps leading up to his A-frame that sat squarely in the middle of nowhere, he *did* need help because his house keys were in his pocket and his hands were full of a giant, slobbering dog.

So, like an idiot, he stood there, at his locked front door, realizing he was going to need help about two seconds after snapping at Sadie that he didn't need any help.

Son of a bitch.

Sadie climbed up the steps and stopped at his side, head cocked, with a sassy smirk curving her luscious mouth. "Problem?"

She had a smirk in her voice, too. Like she didn't already know *exactly* what the problem was. And of course, the dog's tail had started happily swishing at the sound of Sadie's voice and was now smacking Gage in the face with every joyous wag.

"The keys," he muttered.

"Yes?" she intoned sweetly.

"Oh, for God's sake, will you please just grab the keys?"

"Well, sure, but only because you asked so nicely. Where are they?"

"Pants pocket. Front left."

Sadie glanced down at the front of his pants and her smirk disappeared. Take that, he thought smugly. *That's right—you have to reach into my pants. Not so smart-assed now, are you?* But then she reached a tentative hand forward, her eyes still on his crotch, and when she swallowed hard and her little pink tongue darted out to swipe over her lower lip, he didn't feel so smug anymore.

The most beautiful woman he'd ever seen in real life was about to stick her hand in his pants and he had to somehow appear unaffected because they were "starting over" and were just supposed to be friends.

OK, he thought, you can do this. Just think about completely unsexy things. Dead puppies. John Mayer music. That time Adele came to work in yoga pants and a tank top…

And that's when Sadie reached into his front right pants pocket and grabbed his dick.

Fuuuuuccccckkkkk.

"Your other left," he said through clenched teeth.

Her gasp probably sucked all the air out of half the state and she yanked her hand out of his pants so fast it nearly knocked them both off balance. "Holy shit, I'm so sorry," she blurted. "I never meant to do that, I swear to God. I mean, I'm a big supporter of the Me Too movement. I'd never grab anyone without their permission. And I'd never try to take advantage of—"

"Sadie."

She audibly swallowed whatever remaining words she intended to spew on him and glanced up at him guiltily, her face a stunning shade of red. "Yes?"

"Get the fucking keys. Please."

"Sure," she squeaked.

Very gingerly and quickly this time, she lifted his keys out of his pocket—the front *left*, for fuck's sake—and unlocked and opened the door.

Gage walked in ahead of her and set the dog down on the couch—it wasn't like a little dog hair would ruin the already beat-to-hell brown leather monstrosity he'd had since his college days—and glanced back at Sadie, who was looking anywhere but at him.

Not that he blamed her. He'd never grabbed anyone's dick, but he imagined eye contact wasn't exactly comfortable after a thing like that.

He glanced around, pleased to see he hadn't left any piles of laundry or dirty dishes anywhere. He wasn't a slob by any means, but his work schedule was pretty demanding most days, and cleaning was damn low on his priority list after a twelve-hour shift.

But the place looked good today, much like it had when he first decided to rent it five years ago. Lots of open space, huge windows, a floor-to-ceiling river rock fireplace, and gleaming hardwood as far as the eye could see. It only had one bedroom—a loft that overlooked the huge open-concept living room/kitchen/dining room combo— but that suited Gage just fine. It wasn't like he intended to have guests. Like, ever.

But now he had not one, but *two* guests. Which meant he'd have to give Sadie the loft—because, *gentleman*—and share the couch with the dog.

He couldn't allow himself to get anywhere near Sadie after the whole dick-grabbing episode. He pretty much needed to very clearly move Sadie to the friend zone in his mind and quit thinking of her as the most beautiful woman he'd ever seen in real life.

Which meant no more hand-holding, and no sexy thoughts of *any* kind around her. He needed to start thinking of her as one of the guys. Not that he had guy friends, but if he did, he certainly wouldn't be thinking sexy thoughts about any of them.

Out of nowhere, Sadie said, "You have a lovely penis." Then her eyes widened, horrified, and she quickly corrected, "Home! You have a lovely *home*."

Annnnddddd now he was hard. Because *that's* what happens when a gorgeous woman compliments your penis, even if it's an accidental compliment, and even though she's thoroughly friend-zoned you.

His chin hit his chest and he exhaled slowly. So much for thinking of Sadie as one of the guys.

CHAPTER SEVEN

Sadie knew three things she hadn't known before today. Number one, Gage dressed right. Number two, he was a big man. Everywhere. And number three, it apparently *wasn't* possible to die of embarrassment, because if it was, she'd be, well, dead right now.

"You have a lovely penis," she muttered, punching her pillow with way more enthusiasm then was necessary.

What the fuck was wrong with her? It was the middle of the night, she was beyond exhausted, and she still couldn't let go of how badly she'd managed to humiliate herself with Gage. Again.

Part of the problem, she decided as she sat up in bed, was that she was laying in his bed. The sheets were clean, but they still smelled like him. Tide laundry detergent and Iris Spring soap. No fancy colognes or expensive body washes. Just soap on warm male skin. It was arguably the best smell in the world.

But while it was a delight to her senses, it didn't do a damn thing to help relax her brain and let her sleep.

Maybe grabbing a little comfort food would help. A little ice cream would probably do the trick. She was pretty sure she'd noticed a pint of Chubby Hubby in Gage's freezer earlier, which was a little weird, given that he was ridiculously fit. How did someone who had, like, zero percent body fat eat Chubby Hubby and stay all tight and firm and muscle-y?

And this train of thought was also not helping her in any way.

Struggling out of her nest of blankets—seriously, Gage must have given her every blanket he owned to make sure she was comfortable—and made her way downstairs as quietly as possible without bothering to put her robe on. After all, Gage was probably sleeping like a baby, completely unaffected by her presence in his house, the bastard.

And there was, of course, the fact that he'd seen her bare ass today. No reason to be shy about a tank top and flannel Eeyore pants.

But Gage wasn't sleeping. She found him at the front window, staring out into the woods that surrounded his house. He turned when he heard her and her breath caught in her throat.

With his dark hair streaked with silvery moonlight and his flannel shirt open, he looked like he'd walked straight out of an Abercrombie and Fitch catalog and into her wildest fantasy. She tore her gaze away from his chest and noticed the top button of his jeans was undone.

Son of a bitch. This could get bad. Anything—literally *anything*—could come out of her mouth right now. New heights of humiliation could be reached if she didn't get out of here.

But her feet refused to heed her brain's red-alert siren, and she stayed rooted to the floor, staring at him like an idiot.

"You OK?" he asked, his voice even rustier—and sexier—than usual.

She nodded. "Couldn't sleep?" she asked, priding herself on not telling him he looked edible in the moonlight, or that she wanted to count his abs with her tongue.

His gaze moved over her tank top before meeting hers again. He jerked his thumb toward the couch. "Your new friend is a bed hog."

Sadie glanced over at Colin Farrell, who was sprawled out, on his back, with all four paws up in the air. No wonder Gage couldn't sleep. Colin took up at least 75% of the sofa, and it wasn't like Gage was a small man...as she'd discovered firsthand when she'd molested him earlier. (Honestly, she was lucky he wasn't litigious. If he'd filed suit against her, any court in the country would have taken one look at him and labeled her a sexual harasser.)

She slammed the brakes down on that train of thought and shifted her gaze back to the window. "What are you looking at out there?"

"Bear," he said casually.

"No joke?" She scooted across the hardwood floor on her socks and stopped in front of him to get a look. "I've only ever seen bears in the zoo before. Do you get a lot of them here?"

Sure enough, right outside the window, rooting through a half-empty garbage can, was a giant black bear.

Sadie felt Gage lean forward and his warm breath stirred her hair as he said, "Hmm. Pretty much every night."

After determining there was nothing of interest in the can, the bear turned and melted into the trees.

But even a full minute after he disappeared, Sadie didn't move. The heat from Gage's body kept her in place.

That's when it occurred to her that they were totally alone. Civilization was miles away. No neighbors, pitiful phone service…not a single person or situation that could interrupt them tonight.

And they were both single. She also wasn't engaged to his cousin anymore. She'd apologized to Michael long ago, and he was perfectly fine. He'd forgiven her. So, why was it again that she and Gage couldn't be together now? Why did they have to be just friends?

Her mind groped for answers, but came up short.

She was attracted to him, and he was attracted to her. Their timing had been terrible but the attraction—the chemistry, the…*zing*—had always been there. Sadie couldn't imagine that ever going away.

And she hadn't had sex in five long, *long* years. Standing here with a man who looked like the best life-size sex toy ever built after so many years of deprivation was *really* taking a toll on her ability to…brain.

"Gage?" she asked, still looking out the window.

"Hmmm."

"Do you remember when you took care of me when I had food poisoning?"

"Yeah. Why?"

She swallowed hard. "That was the first time I'd ever told anyone about my family. I told you things my brother doesn't even know about me."

She'd told Gage about growing up in the worst trailer park in New Jersey. About how Nick—who'd only been ten—had once stayed awake for three nights in a row, watching over her, clutching his old baseball bat, to keep her mom's drug dealer from crawling into bed with Sadie after their mom passed out like she did every night, high on God-knows-what. About how she used to pray for a family to adopt her—a nice, normal family like *The Brady Bunch*. How she felt guilty for being relieved when her good-for-nothing, abusive parents had died.

And Gage had shared stories with her, too. About his parents. About when his aunt and uncle took him in to keep him out of the foster system. About how he never really felt worthy of their love.

Even Sadie couldn't believe how much they'd shared that night. It had to mean something that they'd felt that comfortable with each other. Right?

There was a pause, but eventually Gage said, "Why me?"

"When I first saw you, I knew you were like me. Former foster kids and orphans…I can always spot them. I'm sure you can, too. It's all in the eyes, you know?"

"Yeah," he said gruffly. "I know."

"The worse the childhood, the older the eyes. And you had old, old eyes, Gage Montgomery." She turned slowly to face him. "Just like me."

His gaze immediately dropped to her mouth. "Michael has young eyes."

She nodded. "Very young eyes. It's probably what I loved most about him. I wanted to be wherever he was because it was obviously a happy, safe place."

"Why'd you leave him then?"

"I finally realized I couldn't run from my past. I didn't have to squeeze myself into a good family and pretend I belonged there in order to be happy. You helped me realize that."

He frowned. "How?"

Crap. He would ask *that*. This was going to be a little embarrassing to admit. But it was too late to back down now. "You grew up just like I did and didn't ever try to be anything you weren't. You didn't change who you were or what you were doing to make other people happy. You were always just...you."

Gage shoved a hand through his hair. "Grace says that makes me a dick."

She snorted. "Sometimes. But no, that's not what I meant. Until I met you, I figured people like us had to act normal—hide our damage—to fit in with a family. But you didn't do that and your family loves you as much as they love Grace and Michael, who are pretty much the happiest, shiniest people I've ever met."

And here came the embarrassing part.

Sadie shifted her gaze down to her toes and murmured, "You taught me that I can be myself—as damaged and broken and messed up as I want to be—and still be worthy of love."

She gasped when he slid his huge, warm hand around the nape of her neck and leaned down so that she was forced to meet his gaze. "You're not damaged or broken or messed-up," he said in a hard voice that belied his gentle touch. "You deserve to have everything you want."

Their faces were so close together that she could see the storm in his eyes, the passion. She licked her parched lips and his gaze dropped to track the movement. "I wanted you," she whispered.

A frown line creased his brow. "What?"

Her heart started pounding loud enough that she was sure he could hear it. "I wanted you from the first moment I saw you." She swallowed hard. "I want you now."

He exhaled sharply and closed his eyes, but didn't step back. "That's a bad idea."

She leaned into him. "Why?"

He opened his mouth to answer, but snapped it shut almost immediately. "I can't remember," he finally answered. "But I know there are a shit ton of reasons why us being together would be a bad idea."

"Do you want me to leave?"

"That's probably a good idea."

But neither of them moved. She reached out and laid tentative hands on his chest. His grip on her neck tightened ever so slightly. When she moved in closer she felt his body tighten and noticed the pressure of his arousal growing against her stomach. Nothing had ever felt better to her.

"Maybe it is a terrible idea," she said. "Me leaving, I mean."

"Yeah?" he asked, his voice sounding like he'd been gargling rusty nails.

"Maybe there's nothing wrong with two young, healthy, *single* people who are attracted to each other...taking what they want," she said quietly. "No strings, no regrets. Just one perfect night."

A muscle in his jaw jumped. "No regrets," he repeated.

"Yeah."

Gage's thumb traced over her jawline, then across her bottom lip. She knew he was probably right and this could be an epically bad idea. But right now, she didn't care. She wanted him too much to worry about anything else, and when he finally—*finally!*—leaned in and pressed his mouth to hers, she almost wept with relief.

The kiss started off softer than she'd imagined it would. It was almost tentative, seeking, but still comforting and...right, somehow. Like finally coming home.

But then she let her hands slide down over the abs she'd had many, *many* dirty fantasies about and pressed her hips against him, and Gage let out a strangled, hungry sound—almost a needy growl. When their lips parted and his tongue tangled with hers, the dam that had been holding back her desperate need for him broke and she let out a hungry growl of her own.

He kept one hand on her neck but curled the other around her hip as their kiss turned dark and wild, a clash of tongues and teeth that left her aching for more.

After what could have been minutes or hours—time lost all meaning when your entire *body* was tingling and even your *goosebumps* had goosebumps—he broke the kiss and pressed his forehead to hers.

"Tell me to stop," he begged.

In that moment, in his arms, in the dark with the real world so

YOU WRECKED ME / Isabel Jordan

far, far away, she would've given him anything. Anything but *that.*

"Don't," she said. "Don't stop. Please."

CHAPTER EIGHT

This couldn't actually be happening.

There was no way Sadie was actually here, in his arms, with her tongue in his mouth, after telling him they should just take what they want from each other. *Just one perfect night.*

And, God, how he *wanted* this night. All the *things* he wanted...

His brain kept trying to remind him this was probably a bad idea, but his libido had pretty much pinned his brain to the ground at this point. He couldn't think about, well, much of *anything* while Sadie's mouth was soft and warm against his, when her body was so close and begging for his touch.

But even so, there was some distant part of him—maybe one stubborn brain cell—that knew this was a fucked-up situation. He was making out with his cousin's former fiancée. And Michael had always been more like a brother to him than a cousin. So, in essence, Gage was violating the bro code—in an *extreme* way—by going after Michael's ex. There was just no way to sugarcoat that.

And that same distant part of him knew their time together would be limited. She traveled the globe for her job and he would likely settle in Chicago to be close to Grace and Nick when the baby was born.

But right now? He couldn't bring himself to care about all of that. Right now, he was kissing the woman of his dreams. And more importantly, she was kissing him back.

The real problem here was that she was just so goddamned pretty. Every time he thought he'd gotten used to those navy eyes, the long, elegant curve of her neck, the shape of her rosy, kissable mouth, she proved him wrong. She looked better every time he saw her.

Which was a little concerning because if he wasn't careful, this could be over tragically, embarrassingly fast. She was too gorgeous, too open and trusting, too warm and caring, too…everything.

And she was looking up at him like she wanted him as much as he wanted her. How was that even possible?

Plus, it had been *way* too long since he'd last had sex. It had been…shit, had it been five years? Yep, he realized. He hadn't had sex since before he first met Sadie.

At this point, he was probably only about two seconds away from losing control completely, tossing her over his shoulder caveman-style and carting her off to his bed to pillage and plunder like a fucking Viking, for God's sake. That's not what Sadie deserved.

He slid his hands down to her backside, mindful of her wound, which had to be stinging like a bitch now that the lidocaine had worn off, and pulled her harder against him, letting her feel how much he wanted her, how hard she made him.

"Tell me you really want this," he said against her mouth. "That you won't wake up tomorrow and regret this."

She reached up and brushed her fingertips over his lower lip.

"I want this. No regrets."

He closed his eyes and let out a relieved breath. "Thank God."

That was all he needed to hear and the rest of his thoughts fled. He was pretty sure if he said anything else it wouldn't be coherent—just a jumbled mess of dirty talk and pleas and gratitude—so he kept his mouth shut to keep from embarrassing herself. Instead, he slid his hands to her waist and pulled her tank top over her head.

Her breasts were perfect—full and round, just large enough to fill his hands. He couldn't hold back a guttural groan. "Fuck, look at you."

"God, yes," she breathed when he bent to suck on one taut peak, then the other.

Sadie reached up and shoved his unbuttoned shirt off his shoulders, then threw her arms around him, pressing those perfect breasts against his bare chest and crushing her mouth to his again. He wrapped his arms around her back and lifted her off the ground. Her long, toned legs immediately came up and locked around his waist. It was like they'd done this dance a million times before, maybe in another life.

She gasped and tightened her grip on his waist as he started moving toward the staircase to the loft. "You can't carry me all the way up the stairs!"

He scoffed. "Watch me."

And she did. Her eyes widened with every step. Apparently she didn't realize he'd carry her up hundreds of flights of steps—barefoot over broken glass, across bear territory, under enemy fire—to get her into his bed.

When they made it to the edge of the bed and he got ready to tip her back against the blankets, she gasped and said, "Wait! I can't do this."

Fuuuccckkk.

He *knew* it'd been too good to be true.

He swallowed hard. "I understand. It's all happening too fast. It's OK to have second thoughts."

She eased back to look up at him, brow furrowed before she let out an exasperated sigh. "Oh, for God's sake! I'm not having second thoughts. I'm saying I can't be on my back because the cut on my ass is stinging like a bitch."

"So…your only problem with this is that you can't be on your back?"

"Yes!"

"You aren't telling me to stop?"

She frowned at him. "Don't be stupid. We just can't do this with me on my back. We'll have to get creative."

His brain locked up. Ahhh…so many creative scenarios, so little time…

His mouth curved into a wicked grin. "I can do creative."

CHAPTER NINE

Gage's smile was pure, unadulterated sin, and the raw, primal need in his eyes gave Sadie pause. What if she didn't live up to his expectations?

Sadie'd had exactly one sexual partner in her life, and that was Michael. They'd both been clueless virgins when they met, so their encounters, while pleasurable, could hardly be described as adventurous or wildly passionate. Something told her Gage was no fumbling virgin and that anything short of wicked and wildly passionate wasn't in his repertoire.

But she didn't have much time to contemplate her nerves when his lips sealed over hers once more. He set her on her feet and they somehow managed to shed the rest of their clothes without breaking the kiss.

Before she could comprehend his intentions, he sank to the mattress, laid down on his back, and pulled her up his body, gripping her hips and guiding her until her knees were on either side of his head, her core a scant inch above his mouth.

"Oh!" She let out a gasp when she realized what he intended to do. A twinge of embarrassment penetrated her lust-fogged brain. She was *so* wet. Surely he wouldn't… "You don't have to do…that."

He gripped her tighter when she started to move off him. "Oh, sweetheart, yes. I *have* to do this." Reaching up, he teased her tight nipples with a light touch she felt all over her body.

All. Over.

"Jesus," he said on a groan. "Look at this view."

And as she looked down at him, at his beautiful mouth, those perfect lips closing over her clit, she had to agree. The view was nothing short of stunning. Earth-shattering and mind-altering in an I'm-now-ruined-for-all-other-men kind of way.

Her legs started to tremble as he flicked her clit with his tongue again and again, and she was starting to make so much noise that she was glad Gage lived in the middle of nowhere. If he had neighbors close by, they'd probably be calling the cops right now, thinking he must be killing her.

And he was. Killing her, that is. The sounds he was drawing from her…they were sounds she was sure she'd never made in her life. Raw, uninhibited noises—noises that up until tonight she thought only existed in porn—that she'd probably be embarrassed about with anyone else. But something told her there was no need to be embarrassed with Gage.

He slid his hand down, teasing her slick entrance with one finger, then two. Her eyes rolled back into her head and her back arched. He hummed a growly, satisfied noise of his own that vibrated along her skin as he continued to taste and torment her, sucking and licking, his tongue far more talented than she ever could have imagined, his fingers reaching a spot—*the* spot—that only Chris

Hemsworth had reached up until that point.

Every muscle in her body tensed as pure pleasure skated along her nerve endings. She cried out, loud enough that the sound echoed like a gunshot in the otherwise quiet room.

But Gage didn't seem to mind. "Yes, sweetheart, let it go. Come for me."

Then he put his mouth back on her and curled his fingers, skillfully stroking that spot—*God, yes, there!*—until her mind completely blanked and all she could do was scream his name as she came so hard she thought she might pass out.

A groan rumbled through Gage and his muscles tensed beneath her, letting her know he was getting off on *her* getting off, which turned her on even more than she was already was.

When she slid down his body and collapsed bonelessly on top of him, gasping and trembling, her mind a glorious, pleasure-soaked blank, he gently gripped her hair in his fist and gave her head a little tug so that she was forced to raise her mouth to his. He kissed her hard, desperate, like he was afraid she was a dream that would dissipate at any minute.

He shifted to kiss her neck, then wrapped an arm around her waist and deftly flipped her over. "On all fours, sweetheart," he growled in her ear.

"All fours?" she asked, trying to beat back her shyness again. She'd never had sex like that before.

"I'd rather have you under me this time, but until that cut doesn't hurt anymore, this angle will let me touch you everywhere and

YOU WRECKED ME / Isabel Jordan

fuck you as hard as you want me to without hurting you."

Holy God. A needy gasp escaped her. Had anything ever sounded that perfect? She didn't think so. And he'd said *this time*. Like they'd have many more times together. *That* sounded even better.

He helped lift and situate her, then tucked a pillow under her hips for support.

She took a deep breath, settled into position, and ignored the little niggling voice in the back of her mind that told her she should be embarrassed to be on all fours like this, with her ass in the air in front of the most perfect-looking man she'd ever seen. But libido trumped embarrassment, it would seem.

Gage made a raw, hungry sound that made her shiver. Sadie glanced back at him over her shoulder and found his gaze fixed firmly on her ass. "If I last two minutes when I'm in you, it'll be a miracle," he said.

She gathered up every ounce of sass she had left and gave him a smirk. "I guess you'll owe me one then."

He leaned over and grabbed a condom from the bedside table, then ran a fist over his erection. "I can do better than *one*," he promised.

Sadie didn't doubt *that* for a minute. Something told her she was going to be sore, limp as a used dishrag, and dehydrated at the end of this night.

And she could hardly wait.

She licked her lips as she watched him roll the condom on, watched him settle on his knees behind her. Gasped as she felt him slide his fingers over her slick flesh.

"Hmmm. So wet," he murmured, almost like he was talking to himself. "So perfect."

Sadie was pretty sure she was going to explode if he didn't move soon. The anticipation—and her nerves, if she was being totally honest—were killing her. But then he wrapped his big body around hers and trailed kisses down her spine, and she wasn't sure her nerves could take *that*, either. It was all too overwhelming, too good.

He was too overwhelming, too good.

Gage slid into her slowly—agonizingly, torturously, *glacially* slow—inch by inch, stretching her, branding her, lighting her body up like a Roman candle, all while maintaining eye contact, since she hadn't been able to stop looking at him over her shoulder.

A moan fell from her lips when he filled her completely. "Oh, God, yes," she panted. "You feel so good."

She saw his jaw tighten and his neck muscles flex as he took a deep breath, almost like he was willing himself to take his time, to make it last.

Sadie was prepared to yell at him that she didn't want his restraint, that she didn't give a *fuck* about making it last. She was far too needy for that. But that's when he reached around and slid his fingertips over the exact place he'd tormented with his mouth earlier—and speaking, let alone yelling, became impossible. So did eye contact. She dropped her forehead to the bed and tried to breathe as pleasure zinged wildly through her entire body.

Then he started to move, slowly at first—in and out, in and

out—then harder, faster, until he gripped her hips and angled even deeper. Her elbows and knees trembled and all she could do was fist the sheets and rock back toward him, holding on for dear life and helping him hit that spot that felt like heat and heaven and sin all wrapped up in one. Over and over again he hit that spot while his fingers kept working their magic.

"Gage…"

"Christ," he said, sounding like his jaw was clenched tight. "You're so fucking tight. So damned beautiful. You need to come for me. Now."

"I—"

Whatever she was going to say was lost to a loud moan as she came so hard her vision went blurry. Every muscle in her body tensed and contracted through the wave of her orgasm, animalistic sounds fell from her lips, and still he didn't let up, slamming into her again and again, his movements sure and confident.

But she knew his control was unraveling. She could hear it in the hitch of his breath, could feel it in the way his hand tightened on her hip. Had he been without sex for as long as she had? How was it even *possible* to look like he looked and go without sex? Surely women were throwing themselves at him daily.

She didn't have long to contemplate that, though, because he hooked an arm around her waist to hoist her up higher and steady her as he pumped into her harder. And when they were both soaked with sweat, when her throat was painfully sore from screaming his name, when she wondered if she'd be able to even walk the next day, he leaned over her, buried his head in her hair and came with a possessive, feral growl that almost had her purring like a satisfied kitten in response.

Rather than collapse on top of her, Gage quickly rolled off her back and flopped down next to her as they both struggled to catch their breath. She heard him dispose of the condom in the wastebasket beside the bed and wondered how he'd found the energy to even complete that small task. He'd just worked *really* hard, after all.

Sadie shoved a hank of sweat-soaked hair off her forehead and whispered, "Wow. I thought sex like *that* only happened in books and movies."

Gage pushed up on his elbow and stared down at her. He leaned over and kissed the tip of her nose so gently Sadie suddenly felt like crying and said, "It's not usually like that. That was all you."

She shook her head. "No way. That had to be you, because I've never had *that* before."

He grunted. "It definitely wasn't all me, sweetheart."

Sadie was exhausted, but did her best to give him a saucy smile. "Well, there's only way to know for sure."

His eyes darkened a split second before he grabbed her and shifted her so that she straddled him. "Round two it is," he said in that rumbly voice that never failed to weaken her knees.

She was about to protest that she couldn't possibly go again so soon, but when she wiggled against him and felt him getting hard beneath her, she realized her error.

Huh. Turns out I can go again so soon. Who knew?

CHAPTER TEN

Sadie woke up starfished across Gage on one side of his bed. She glanced over and realized that at some point during the night, Colin Farrell had made his way up the stairs and crawled into bed with them. He was currently taking up the other half of the bed, laying on his back with his front legs up in the air again.

And Gage was right. Colin Farrell snored like a bear. A congested bear. A congested bear with asthma and a deviated septum.

Gage didn't snore, though, she realized. His breaths were deep and even, telling her he was still sound asleep. Not surprising. He'd worked *very* hard the previous night. All night, actually.

Very. Hard.

He'd given her orgasm after orgasm like it was his damn job, then they'd both dropped off into exhausted, spent, sweaty slumber sometime right before dawn.

Sadie would never admit it aloud because it made her sound all kinds of pathetic, but it had been the best night of her life. She hadn't felt so free and uninhibited and *wanted*—no, *needed*—since, well, ever. For some reason, whether it was their similarly crappy upbringings, or their crazy, off-the-charts physical chemistry, Sadie felt more like *herself* with Gage than with anyone else in her life.

Aaannnddd now she sounded all kinds of pathetic again.

Why was the one man who made her feel like she could be herself no matter what, a) her ex-fiancé's cousin, b) a grumpy recluse who lived and worked in the middle of nowhere, and c) not exactly someone who was known for building emotional relationships with *anyone?*

The odds were stacked against them in pretty much every conceivable way. She'd told him she wouldn't have any regrets, but now she wasn't so sure. If last night had been their one and only time together and they were forced to go their separate ways today, would she be OK with that?

She'd have to be, she realized, even though the thought of leaving Gage now made her stomach clench.

And even worse, she had no idea how he was feeling. It wasn't like they'd talked much last night. Unless *talking* included shared words of the "oh, God, yes, right there" and "ride me harder, faster" variety, that is. They'd done plenty of *that* kind of talking.

But wasn't this what she always did? Get way too attached way too soon in an effort to force a relationship, a bond with someone—anyone—who might love her and never leave her? Were her feelings for Gage some kind of remnant of her old abandonment issues and emotional baggage?

Her pathetic, hand-wringing musings were interrupted by her phone, which started blaring *Bad Company* (the *5 Finger Death Punch* version, of course) at a totally unreasonable volume for someone who'd had next to nothing in the way of sleep for the past 48 hours to handle.

She lifted up, fully prepared to crawl off Gage and grab her phone, but he mumbled something she didn't quite catch into her hair and grabbed hold of her hips in a grip that told her moving wasn't currently an option. So instead, she leaned up and over, which put her boobs firmly in Gage's face—*God, please don't let me smother him in his sleep with my boobs*—and snatched her phone off the nightstand, not even bothering to check caller ID.

"Hello?" she snarled grumpily.

There was a pause on the other end of the line, then her brother said, "Well, good morning to you, too, sunshine."

Ugh. Of course it was her brother. Nick was a morning person. Always had been. He was alert and cheerful every day at 5 a.m. and didn't even drink coffee. Bastard. Sadie was only half-alert at 9 after drinking a full pot of the black gold that was her life blood and best friend.

"What's going on, Nicky? It's early."

He chuckled, no doubt at her expense since her sleep-roughened voice made her sound like a three-packs-a-day chain smoker. "I just wanted to check on you. Grace told me what you did yesterday."

For a second she panicked. What she *did* yesterday? She was *laying* on top of *what she did yesterday*! *What she did yesterday* currently had some impressive morning wood that was poking her. If given half an opportunity, *what she did yesterday* would become what she'd do *today*, over and over again if possible.

Then it occurred to her foggy, coffee-less brain that Grace couldn't possibly know that she'd seduced Gage. Nick was probably just referring to her injury.

"Um…yeah," she said, trying to keep any trace of I-had-lots-of-athletic-sex-last-night out of her voice. That wasn't the kind of thing she wanted to discuss with her *brother*, for God's sake. "It was just a stupid accident. I'm fine today." And she was. The cut on her ass didn't even sting anymore.

"Good. Did Gage treat you alright?"

Did he ever! Especially when he did that thing with his tongue on her…

She gave herself a sharp mental slap and said, "He's great." Shit! Her voice sounded totally dreamy and smitten when she'd said that. "I mean, he *was* great." *Double shit! That sounded even worse.* "He has great hands." *And a great tongue, and a magic penis, and abs that she could scrub her shirts on, and…gah! This just kept getting worse.* "I mean, he's a great doctor and I'm fine today. How are you?"

Another pause on his end. "I'm fine. Sadie, are you sure you're OK?"

"Yes. Why do you ask?"

"Because you sound a little…"

"Caffeine-free?" she suggested.

"Fucking crazy," he countered.

Mental sigh. "Same difference," she muttered.

He chuckled again and started telling her about something that had happened to him at work recently. He was an air marshal, and normally, she loved hearing stories about the types of insanity he encountered on a daily basis. But this morning, she found herself struggling to pay attention, and her lack of caffeine didn't have a single thing to do with it.

Beneath her, Gage shifted, obviously waking up, and shoved one hand into her hair at her nape, tightening his grip on her hip with the other. Then he gently tugged her head to one side and ran the tip of his tongue over the ultra-sensitive spot just below her ear. Her eyes fluttered shut and she couldn't contain the shuddering sigh that slipped past her lips.

"Sadie?" Nick asked. "Are you OK?"

The hand Gage had on her hip slid up and palmed her breast. "I'm so, so good," she said thickly, and she felt his smile against her neck.

That's when she realized Gage was *enjoying* making her lose her train of thought—and her mind—while her brother was right there and could possibly hear any sex noises she might make. Ugh! He really was an asshole sometimes. A ridiculously sexy asshole with some well-hidden nice-guy tendencies, but an asshole nonetheless.

Well, two could play *that* game.

Sadie slid her hand down his side slowly, teasingly, then around his hip, not stopping until she had a firm grip on that truly impressive morning wood. His entire body tensed beneath her, and she bit back a triumphant grin. Gotcha!

But then he shifted and slid his thigh between hers, forcing her to straddle him fully. She gasped when he gripped her hips and moved her back and forth a little. God, the pressure their position put on her clit was *perfect*. So fucking perfect.

"What's so fucking perfect?" Nick asked, obviously confused.

Fuck! She'd said that out loud! "Um…Nick, can I call you back after…" *I've come on Gage's dick a few times?* "…I've had some coffee…or something?" Heavy on the *or something*.

He sighed. "Yeah. Probably a good idea. You're a zombie this morning. Give me a call after ten. Grace and I should be back from her prenatal checkup by then."

Sadie ended the call with mumbled agreements and dropped her phone on the floor. "God," she moaned, moving against him, "what are you trying to do to me?"

He wrapped his arms around her. "If you don't know, then I'm not doing it right."

Oh, he was doing it right. She would've told him so, too, but he cut her off when he put his hands on either side of her face and pulled her lips down to his for a warm, hard kiss.

He groaned as she started rocking against him again, insistently, urgently. Then she returned his groan when he grabbed her hips and pressed her harder against him.

Then a thought hit her—a horrible, *terrible* thought—and it almost made her cry. "We used all the condoms last night," she whispered.

He kissed her again, then slipped his fingers into her hair, bunching it up in his fists. "Can you get off like this?"

To punctuate his question, he rolled his hips against hers and a loud, embarrassing moan escaped her. His answering noise was something between a chuckle and a growl. "I'll take that as a yes," he muttered. "You keep moving like that, using me, and I get to see you come…um…yeah, that's all it'll take for me, too, sweetheart."

The fact that he could get off on *her* getting off turned her on almost more than the friction she was creating between them. Almost.

So, she let go of any lingering self-consciousness left in her and picked up her pace, rocking against him hard, with complete abandon.

"Look at me," he said on a moan beneath her. "I want to see and feel and hear you when you come. Give me everything."

She lifted her eyes to his and the intensity and heat she saw there was enough to push her over the edge. But she wanted him to come with her, so she grabbed his hips and ground against him harder, increasing the pressure between them. She felt the moment he lost control, felt it in the tightening of his muscles beneath her, saw it in his eyes as he ruthlessly held her gaze.

He shouted her name as he came, and Sadie cried out her release right along with him.

Sadie's heart raced and her muscles trembled as she dropped limply to his chest and pressed her face into the spot where his neck met his shoulder. She knew she should move off him and grab a towel to clean up the sticky mess between them, but she couldn't care less about that at the moment. She was too blissed out.

Gage didn't seem to care about the mess either as his arms banded tightly around her. She smiled when he kissed the top of her head.

"Good morning," she murmured.

"Fuck yeah it is," he said, his voice still rough from sleep.

She couldn't hold back a girly giggle, and his body shook beneath her with the force of his own laughter when that girly giggle turned into a snort.

Eventually their laughs quieted, but they stayed that way, entwined and sated until Gage slid his hands up her spine, into her hair and asked, "You good?"

There was a certain weight to his words and a tension settling into his muscles that told her he wasn't asking her if, say, she was hungry or if she'd slept OK. Something told her he was asking if she was regretting anything they'd done or said to each other throughout the night and morning.

"I'm good," she answered quietly. "I'm really, *really* good."

Some of the tension left his body and she thought she felt him smile into her hair a split second before he jackknifed to a sitting position, then twisted his legs out of the bed and stood up, taking her with him while she clung to him like a tree sloth. She let out a little squeal and locked her ankles around his waist so that he wouldn't drop her.

"What the hell are you doing?" she asked on a gasping laugh.

"I'm taking you into the shower to see if I can upgrade that *good* to *great.*"

She laughed all the way to the bathroom, but in the end, about an hour and three orgasms later, Sadie could definitely confirm that

Gage was a man of his word, and her *good* had for sure been upgraded to *great.*

CHAPTER ELEVEN

"Miss Sadie!"

Gage shook his head as yet another person he barely knew greeted and hugged Sadie. She'd been in town a handful of days and the breakfast crowd at the diner greeted her like she was Norm strolling into *Cheers*. He'd seen half these people at the hospital over the past five years and he barely rated a chin lift or a finger wave from any of them.

"Miss Mabel," Sadie said with a sweet, dimpled smile that made Gage's heart clench up a little. "How's your back feeling today?"

The sixty-year-old waitress beamed at Sadie like a proud momma. "Oh, it's a bit better today, darlin', thank you for asking." Then she turned a glare on Gage. "Not that *he* cares. Didn't do a thing other than write me a prescription and tell me to lose weight."

Not that Gage would discuss a patient's case in public, but his inner asshole wanted to ask Mabel what she'd expected. She was a woman who spent all day on her feet, and she was only five-one and weighed more than Gage did. Why *wouldn't* her back hurt?

He'd given her a prescription for some anti-inflammatories, ordered some X-rays that she never came in for, and advised her that losing some weight and getting her BMI back into a normal range for someone her height might take some pressure off her body. What else was he supposed to do?

But he didn't have to say anything, because Sadie immediately came to his defense telling Mabel, "Come on, Miss Mabel, I'm sure it wasn't like that. He's a great doctor! Did you know that Gage graduated top of his class at Johns Hopkins?"

Her glare turned into a sour frown. "No. But I'm guessing their grading scale didn't include bedside manner."

Nope, Gage inwardly agreed. It sure hadn't. Thank God.

Sadie gave the woman a frown. "I'm sure Gage was just doing his best to take care of you. He was *very* good to me yesterday. I thought his bedside manner was just *fine*."

He lifted a brow at her. Just *fine*? He'd show her *just fine* when he got her away from her adoring public.

She gave him a sassy smile before turning back to Miss Mabel. "And he even helped that poor stray dog I found. I'm sure Walter told you all about him, right?"

Mabel's expression seemed to soften up a bit at the mention of Colin Farrell. She sniffed and conceded, "Yes. I'd heard about that. It was a kind thing to do."

Sadie slid into the booth across from Gage and turned that mega-watt smile of hers on him. It was twice as effective straight-on as it had been when she was offering it to Miss Mabel. Shit. He wasn't sure his heart could take too much of *that*.

Mabel's gaze shifted between them like she was watching a tennis match. "You two kids are out awfully early...together."

The emphasis she put on together was decidedly suggestive, Gage decided. But Sadie seemed to ignore it as she answered, "Yep. We had to drop the dog off at the vet's office for a quick check-up, so we thought we'd stop in for breakfast while we waited."

Gage could see the wheels turning in Mabel's brain. It didn't take her too long to connect the dots. Gage could tell the second she decided that he and Sadie were more than just casual acquaintances.

"So…you two are…here *together?*"

As if the two of them sitting at the same table and Sadie defending him wasn't clue enough. Again, Gage's inner asshole wanted to give her a firm, "Duh." But for Sadie's sake, he didn't.

Sadie answered patiently, without sarcasm or snark of any kind. Then after they'd ordered—a short stack of buttermilk pancakes and bacon for her, oatmeal with fresh blueberries for him—Mabel shuffled off to the kitchen, pausing just long enough to glare over her shoulder at Gage one last time.

Sadie shook her head and grinned at him. "You weren't kidding, were you? You really haven't made any friends here."

He shrugged. "Didn't seem important. I'm a short timer here. In fact, my time's up in about a month."

"Where will you go after that?"

"Haven't decided yet. Figure I'll eventually end up in Chicago to be close to Grace and Nick when the baby's born. Thank God they left LA." He shuddered. "Don't think I could've survived there. What about you?"

He watched her toying with the sugar packets and held his

breath waiting for her to answer. He didn't want to admit it, but hearing her say she planned to keep living an amazing, jet-setting life abroad, connecting with people, making friends, while he settled in one city and went back to surgery, where it was acceptable—encouraged, even—not to connect with anyone, made him inexplicably anxious. They were so different. They made absolutely no sense together.

So why did it feel like he was about to lose something he'd never even really had?

She lifted her eyes to his, looking as nervous as he felt. "Well...I know the timing of this is going to sound weird, and I swear, I'm not stalking you or anything...but even before last night, I'd been thinking of establishing a home base. I mean, I love my column, don't get me wrong. But all the travel is starting to weigh on me. And I was thinking maybe I should settle in Chicago, too. Nicky's the only family I have, you know?" When he didn't respond, she started talking faster, "And now I have a dog to think about. I can't really travel all over with Colin Farrell. It wouldn't be any kind of life for a dog. And I could always do freelance writing, or start work on a book, or, really, the possibilities are endless, I guess. And I don't want this to make you feel weird. I know we said one night and that this was casual, and I'm good with that, I swear. I just—"

Gage reached across the table and scooted the bowl of sugar packets away from her before grabbing her hand and lacing his fingers through hers. "Sadie, stop," he said.

She blew out a breath. "Thank you."

He smiled, but couldn't keep from saying, "You're totally

stalking me, aren't you?"

She snorted. "You're such an asshole." But she said it with a smile, telling him she didn't mind too much.

He gestured to the regular diner crowd, who wasn't even pretending to give them privacy. "I think we've established that. Which is probably why everyone is looking like they want to rescue you from me."

Sadie was up, around the table, and in his lap before Gage could blink. She wrapped her arms around his neck and gave him a quick, hard kiss. "Well, this should let them know I don't need—or want—to be rescued," she whispered against his mouth.

Gage wasn't used to having people stand up for him, especially not big-hearted, genuinely *good* people like Sadie. The fact that she thought he was worthy of that kind of protection…it was humbling. And it made his chest tight and caused some kind of weird lump of emotion to clog his throat.

She was wrecking him. She'd taken a sledgehammer to all the walls he'd built around himself over the years. And the scariest part?

He could totally get used to it.

Something told him, he already *had* gotten used to it, and if he let her go now without telling her how he felt, he'd regret it forever.

When he didn't say anything, she leaned back and frowned down at him. "I didn't embarrass you, did I?"

She moved to stand up and he banded his arms around her, holding her in place. "I don't need casual," he blurted.

Her brow furrowed. "Excuse me?"

"You said…last night could just be about two people taking what they want from each other. Casual. No regrets, right?"

"Yes," she said hesitantly, drawing the word out for a few extra syllables.

"I don't need casual. I want to get to know you better. See more of you. See *lots* of you." He blew out a frustrated breath and shoved a hand through his hair. "That sounded dirty. I didn't mean it to sound dirty. I'm saying…shit, I don't even know what I'm trying to say anymore. I'm not good at this. At any of it. But, I guess… I don't just want a one-night stand with you. I want more."

She stared down at him for what felt like an awkward eternity, then bit her lower lip, looking all kinds of confused. "I don't…I don't know what to do with…all that."

Well, *that* kind of felt like a knife to the heart. Lovely. "You don't know what you want—or you don't know what you want with *me?*"

For a second, she looked like a trapped animal, wild-eyed and ready to bolt. But then she blew out a deep breath and started spewing words again. "Look, its way more complicated than that for me, OK? I've always been too quick to give my heart away. My therapist—I went to one after the whole wedding fiasco—said that because of my childhood issues, I'm an extreme people pleaser, and that I cling to people—men, in particular— so that I don't ever have to be alone again. I did everything in my power to make Michael happy, to the point that I didn't even know who I was anymore. I mean, I starved myself to lose weight because the girl he dated before me was a toothpick and I assumed that was the look he liked. I completely lost myself in that relationship. I would've done *anything* to worm my way into his family—your family. So, my heart is telling me that I don't just want a casual relationship with you, either, but how can I trust my heart when it's made so many bad choices up until now? How do I know that if I started a real relationship with you that I wouldn't just be falling back into my old patterns? How would we—"

Gage cupped her face in his hands and said, "Stop."

She swallowed whatever else she'd been about to say and whispered, "Thank you."

He did his best to ignore the sinking feeling in his heart caused by knowing Sadie might not ever want a relationship with him, that she might just be perfectly happy with their one night together and never pursuing anything more than that. After all, it wasn't like he had any experience with relationships, either. Even if she did decide to get seriously involved with someone, he probably wasn't the safest bet anyway.

"I understand," he told her.

"Really?" She let out a mirthless chuckle. "That's great because I'm not sure I do."

He actually *wasn't* 100% sure he understood, but she hadn't told him to fuck off and leave her alone, so he was taking that as a win. "How about we slow down, back up, and go back to your original idea about being friends?"

Friends who'd fucked like rabbits all night. Sure. Why not?

The relief on her face wasn't another knife to the heart. It was more like a knee to the nuts. "That sounds great," she said. "Maybe in time…"

She trailed off and he didn't push for more. Yes, in time, if he was the luckiest bastard in the world, maybe they could be something other than friends who saw each other naked that one time. But he wasn't going to hold his breath. Lucky had never really been his thing.

Then she smiled at him, and it was so warm that it sparked something he hadn't felt in a long, *long* time. If he hadn't missed his guess, he'd say that feeling was…hope.

Fucking hope. Of all the feelings he could have in this moment, *that* was the absolute worst. Nothing was as devastating as watching shit fall apart after you'd had *hope* for a different ending.

Yep. It was official. She was totally wrecking him.

CHAPTER TWELVE

They did their best to ignore the curious stares of pretty much the entire town as they ate breakfast.

Well, she wasn't sure if what he was eating could even be *called* breakfast. It was way too healthy for that. But, she imagined eight-packs like Gage's weren't made of pancakes and bacon, so she didn't tease him about it.

Not *too* much, anyway.

While they ate and ignored the chatter around them, they talked, and for Sadie, that was almost as good as the entire night had been. *Almost*, because, the sex had been fifty shades of OHHOLYGOD. But still, the talking was amazing because it made her think their connection five years ago wasn't a fluke. Maybe there really *was* something between them that wasn't the result of hot physical chemistry and all her messed-up emotional baggage…

She mentally told herself to snap out of it. They were firmly back in the friend zone now. Her heart just couldn't be trusted at the moment, and she needed to stop looking for evidence that what they had together was real and worth pursuing long-term.

Even if being with him was more of a rush than any assignment she'd ever been on for *Luxe*. Even if she never found anyone who made her feel as alive as Gage did.

Even if she was incapable of loving someone and letting herself be loved ever again.

God, she was getting maudlin. Time to lighten up those dark thoughts, she told herself.

She was about to ask him a question of the utmost importance—whether or not he agreed that country music was the work of the devil—when she got a text from Nick.

Sadie glanced down at the text and muttered, "Shit. 911."

Gage's phone pinged at the same time. He glanced down and sighed. "Grace. 912. That's not good."

"What's a 912?"

"More important than 911," he answered, then rolled his eyes as she raised a brow at him. "It's a Grace-ism." He gestured to her phone. "Call him. I'll call her and we'll see what the hell's going on."

Sadie immediately called Nick and stuck her finger in her other ear to drown out the diner noise. He answered on the first ring, which couldn't possibly be a good thing. Nick never answered on the first ring. He was a pick-it-up-a-half-a-heartbeat-before-it-goes-to-voicemail kind of guy.

"What's wrong?" she responded to his breathless mumbled greeting.

"Grace has mild preeclampsia," he said. "It's not a big deal at this point, but she's been put on bedrest until the end of the pregnancy."

Sadie had to gulp back a horrified gasp. She wasn't sure she'd ever even seen Grace *sit* down for more than a minute at a time, let alone *lie* down for days on end. The woman was a force of nature. "How's she taking it?"

"About as well as you'd expect," he answered wryly. "Which is why I called."

"Of course. What can I do?"

"Well, I'm supposed to work next week. I've got back-to-back flights scheduled, but I can't leave Grace alone. She pitched a bitch when I told her I'd cancel and stay with her."

Sadie snorted. "I'll bet. You need me to come stay with her?"

"I know it's a lot to ask." He sighed, and Sadie could just about picture him running his hands through his hair like he always did when he was frustrated. "But she says she'll go nuts with me hovering over her all week when I should be working. And she needs some help setting up the nursery. Having you here is the only compromise we could both agree on."

"Of course I'll come. It's nothing. Don't worry about it at all."

There was a deep, relieved sigh, followed by a loaded pause on the other end of the line. Then, Nick said, "I can't tell you how much I appreciate that, Sades. But, there's something else I need to warn you about. Two things, really."

Well, that sounded ominous. "OK, shoot."

"First of all, Grace is not entirely...herself these days. Pregnancy hormones are no fucking joke. Prepare yourself."

Sadie couldn't hold back a laugh. "Are we talking demon possession? Like, I should stock up on rock salt and holy water? I can probably re-watch season 2 of *Supernatural* on my way there to memorize a few exorcism spells if you think it'll help."

He didn't laugh. "You joke, but don't think I haven't considered rock salt and holy water a few times over the past few months."

She shook her head. "Oh, you're such a baby. I'm not worried about pregnancy hormones. What's the other thing you need to warn me about?"

Another pause before, "Grace is asking Gage to come next week, too, just in case. Is that going to be weird for you?"

Because he's had his tongue on every part of my body? Why would that be weird?

Then she reminded herself that Nick didn't know anything about her and Gage, so she answered, "Of course it won't be weird. We're both adults." *Who had done very, very adult things to each other just last night. And this morning. And once in the car on the way to breakfast.* "And it makes sense that Grace would want her cousin, who just happens to be an amazing doctor, around while she's on bedrest."

"He's an *amazing* doctor, huh?"

His tone was suspicious. Shit! She'd given away too much information. He knew something! She really didn't want to talk to her brother about her sex life. "Well, yeah, I mean, he graduated first in his class and everything, didn't he? I'm no expert, but I think the Johns Hopkins thing is a big deal."

"Sadie," Nick began, sounding all kinds of suspicious, "you don't still have a...crush on Gage, do you?"

If by crush *you mean all-consuming desire for and stalker-like fascination with, then…sure.* She made a *pfffttt* sound. "Of course not. Don't be silly."

"Well, good. That'd be a disaster."

She frowned. "Why would it be a disaster?"

He laughed. "Come on, Sades. *You* and *Gage?* I mean, opposites attract is one thing, but that'd be ridiculous. And Michael would shit a brick."

Crap. Michael. They'd had a few good talks since she pulled her runaway bride maneuver on him, and he sounded sincere when he said he forgave her. But forgiving her and knowing she'd had naughty-naked-fun time with *Gage*…well, *that* was something else entirely.

After a few more minutes of conversation to work out the logistics of everything (including the fact that Colin Farrell would have to come with her…which Nick wasn't entirely happy about, but eventually agreed to), Sadie told her brother she loved him and ended the call. Gage ended his call with Grace a moment later.

"Is Grace OK?" she asked.

"Grace is a disaster," he said without hesitation. "Pregnancy hormones have had their way with her. I don't think I've ever heard her yell and sob at the same time before. It's disconcerting."

"But you told her you'd be there?"

He looked mildly offended that she had to ask. "Of course I did. What else would I do?"

The cold little ball of reality Nick had shoved down her throat with his mention of Michael melted at his words. "You're not nearly as much of an asshole as you'd like everyone to think you are."

He frowned at her, but his eyes were smiling. "Well, thanks. And you don't suck nearly as much as other people do."

"Such a flatterer," she said, struggling—and failing—not to grin at him like an idiot.

"That's me: all flattery all the time."

"So, I guess we're going on a road trip, huh?"

"Guess so. I'll need to work out hospital coverage, but there's a surgeon in Jasper I went to school with who owes me a favor. I'm hoping I can blackmail him into coming down here to cover for a while. And I'm assuming flying with a dog the size of a Shetland pony isn't possible. I'm driving, though."

She raised a challenging brow at him. "As long as I get to pick the music."

He grimaced. "Fine. Not country, though. Anything but that."

Be still my heart.

Now how the hell was she supposed to keep him in the friend zone when he was determined to be so damned perfect for her all the time?

CHAPTER THIRTEEN

Sadie was a writer who, it had been said, had a decent amount of talent, and even she couldn't come up with a better word than *sucks* to describe the drive from Montana to Illinois.

So much of what was between here and there was farm land and desolate stretches of empty highway that Sadie was starting to resent all the big square states in the middle of the map. She could barely distinguish one from the others anymore.

And her butt had gone numb about 200 miles ago, so there was *that*.

But, she thought, glancing over at Gage, at least the scenery on the inside of the car was pretty.

"Stop it," he said, not sparing her a glance.

"Stop what?"

"Looking at me like you've seen me naked."

She smiled. "But I have seen you naked."

"And since we agreed that you won't be seeing me naked again anytime soon, you need to cut it out."

He was right, of course, even if getting naked again with Gage sounded like the best idea she'd heard all day. So Sadie just kept her mouth shut.

She glanced back at Colin Farrell, whose tail thumped joyfully against the seat as he stared out the window, apparently entranced by a field of cows. At least *someone* was enjoying the drive, she supposed.

"I'm bored," she admitted, her tone dangerously close to whiny teenager territory. She was probably only a few minutes away from asking him if they were there yet. "You have to talk to me more."

He glanced over at her, his smartass brow raised. "You're saying you need me to entertain you?"

"Yes. Entertain me. Talk to me about something. I'll give you a topic to start with. Favorite color. Go."

"Blue," he said after a short pause. "Deep navy blue."

Her heart clenched for a minute. Her eyes were navy blue. "I'm kind of partial to blue/green myself," she said quietly. "Pale blue/green, like sea glass."

He turned his pale-like-sea-glass eyes toward her fully for a second, then turned them back to the road. He didn't say anything, but the way his eyes crinkled up at the corners like he was fighting off a smile, told her he understood her game.

"Favorite movie?" he asked her. "Is it still *The Princess Bride*?"

Well, that one was easy. "Of course it is. I've changed a lot over the years, but not the really important stuff like *that*. You? Still *Die Hard*?"

"Of course. Although *The Bourne Identity* gave it a run for its money."

She rolled her eyes. Typical guy answer. "I don't think we ever talked music. Best band of all time?"

He made a *pfffttt* sound. "Queen, of course."

Sadie nodded her approval. "I would have also accepted Aerosmith, and a valid argument could have been made for The Beatles or Audioslave, because, you know, Chris Cornell."

Michael had always said Pearl Jam, which was just wrong. Sure, the music was great, but Sadie had never been able to get past the fact that Eddie Vedder mumbled lyrics instead of singing them. To be able to earn the title of "best ever," you had to be able to actually *understand* what the hell they were saying, in Sadie's opinion.

After that, Sadie and Gage had a rather heated argument regarding who'd had the best claim to the Iron Throne on *Game of Thrones*. Gage thought it had been Dany, but it was obviously Gendry, Robert's bastard, who'd had the best claim.

But they eventually decided they'd just agree to disagree, and that *Game of Thrones* was a highly personal subject—right up there with religion and politics—that shouldn't be discussed unless one *wanted* to pick a fight.

At least they both agreed that Rick should have let Maggie kill Negan on *The Walking Dead*. If they'd disagreed on *that*, Sadie wasn't sure they could have remained friends. That shit would've been *way* too hard to overcome.

There was one other possibly controversial topic that Sadie was wicked curious about. But when she opened her mouth to ask, the words dried up in her throat. What if she didn't really want to hear the answer? Wondering and knowing were sometimes two very different things.

Gage sighed. "Don't be a wimp. Go ahead and ask."

Wimp? Well that was just rude. And a little too *true* for her liking. "How do you know I want to ask you something?"

"You're biting your lower lip. You only do that when you're thinking about asking something you aren't sure you should ask."

Sadie wasn't aware she'd been doing that, but now that he mentioned it…huh. That might be why she all of a sudden tasted blood. "You're not even looking at me. How did you know I was biting my lip?"

The look he pinned her with made her stomach flip and her heart knock against her ribs like it was about to make a break for it. "I'm never *not* looking at you, Sadie," he said in the same sex-soaked, growly whisper that never failed to weaken her knees.

Holy. God.

She swallowed hard. "Stop looking at me like you've seen me naked," she answered, trying for a flip, sassy tone and failing miserably. But if she'd been going for breathy and borderline slutty, well, *that* would've been a slam dunk.

His eyes traveled the length of her, their wicked sparkle clearly indicating that yes, he'd seen her naked and if he had his way, he'd see her naked again. Many, many times and soon.

"Ask," he reminded her when he turned back to the road.

OK, just bite the bullet. Don't be a sissy. "Serious girlfriends? How many and when?" she blurted.

"I've never had a serious girlfriend," he answered without hesitation.

She blinked at him. "Really? How is that possible? Have you *seen* you?"

He shrugged one shoulder. "Never really wanted to get involved long-term, you know? It's the orphan thing, I guess."

Fear of abandonment, Sadie realized. She knew it well. But where Gage decided to avoid grabbing hold of anyone for fear of losing them, Sadie had done the opposite. She'd always been a clinger. Neither coping mechanism was particularly healthy.

Weren't they just the perfect pair of emotional misfits?

"And what about…you know," she said, willing herself not to blush. "How long had it been for you?"

The smartass brow made another appearance, this time accompanied by the smartass smirk. Gage had many, many smartass expressions, Sadie realized. "It had been a little over 5 years since I last *you know'd*."

Well, if *that* wasn't a jaw-dropping statement she didn't know what was. "You mean since before you…"

"Met you?" he supplied when she trailed off. "Yeah. Like I said, I'm never *not* looking at you. I'm an asshole, but I'm not the type of asshole who has sex with one woman while wanting another."

"It'd been five years for me, too," she whispered.

She shrugged when his eyes flew back to hers. She didn't say it, but the implication was clear.

I'm never not looking at you, either, Gage.

That's when he did something that tore her heart wide open. Something that was so stunning in its guilelessness that Sadie's breath stuttered.

He smiled.

There wasn't a hint of snark or smirky-ness in it anywhere. It was open and honest and genuine. It was something she'd never seen him offer another person.

It was *her* smile.

And now she had to somehow keep this man at a safe emotional distance so that she could take things slowly. Stay in the friend zone. Figure out if her feelings for him were real, or just the result of her lifelong patterns. She had to *somehow* not throw herself at this man and ride him like a rodeo bull. Again.

She was sooooooo fucked.

CHAPTER FOURTEEN

The drive from Montana to Illinois took roughly 700 years. The terrain was boring to the point of mind-numbing, rest areas and gas stations were few and far between in many spots, and Colin Farrell had apparently eaten something that didn't agree with him, because the gas he emitted for the majority of the trip could be bottled and used in biological warfare.

If not for Sadie, he would've abandoned his car at the airport in Kansas and flown the rest of the way. Spending time talking to her had been the only positive of the trip.

She was so different from the girl he met all those years ago. She was more mature, more likely to share her thoughts and opinions, and less likely to acquiesce to those around her.

And yet there were times when it seemed she hadn't changed at all. The giggle that ended in a snort when she found something truly hilarious, the wide, friendly smile that hit him in the heart like the sun rising after the longest, darkest night, how she listened in a way that made him feel like they were the only two people left on the planet...those things were all still very much like five-years-ago Sadie.

He'd had a crush on her back then. A crush that was largely rooted in lust, he imagined. But now? He had the distinct impression

YOU WRECKED ME / Isabel Jordan

his feelings were starting to get deeper than his simple crush on her had been.

It was kind of terrifying, if he was being honest with himself. He wasn't used to…caring about anyone but himself and his family. Was he even capable of giving someone like Sadie the kind of love she deserved? Where would he even start? Chances were good that he'd fuck up. A lot.

And, of course, there was the fact that she didn't even want a relationship with him. So, there was *that*.

"Oh, thank you, sweet baby Jesus," Sadie muttered, jumping out of the car in Nick and Grace's driveway before it had come to a full stop. Then she squealed and jumped up and down a few times with her arms in the air like *Rocky*, yelling, "We're here!"

Gage couldn't hold back a sharp bark of laughter as he watched her practically skip up the front steps. He was pretty damn happy to finally be here, too, even if he had no intention of squealing, jumping, or skipping. But watching Sadie do it warmed his cold heart up a few degrees.

Then she turned back to him and tossed that blinding smile of hers his way.

OK, maybe it warmed his heart up more than just a *few* degrees.

Nick answered the door and pulled Sadie into a hug that looked like it had bone-crushing force behind it. But true to form, Sadie hugged her brother back with equal enthusiasm and started telling him about their trip.

Gage carried their bags into the foyer with Colin Farrell trailing happily behind him. He didn't want to interrupt the brother-sister reunion, so he took a moment to appreciate the suburban mansion Grace and Nick had built about forty-five minutes outside of Chicago.

Much like his cousin Grace, the place was beautiful and elegant, yet not at all stuffy or pretentious. The wide, marble-tiled foyer was painted a welcoming, buttery yellow, and from where he stood, Gage could see that it lead to a completely open-concept living space/dining room/kitchen. When the little one was up and walking, Nick and Grace would be able to see him/her from anywhere in the space. Smart.

Sleek leather furniture dotted with colorful, cushy throw pillows and flanked by simple walnut end tables filled the living room, and a giant flat-screen TV decorated the floor-to-ceiling river rock fireplace. It all looked like it had been professionally designed, but yet you could still picture yourself sitting on *that* couch, watching *that* TV, with your feet up on *that* upholstered ottoman.

There was a fancy-looking, iron-railed spiral staircase that led to the upper floor, where he imagined Grace was ensconced.

Nick let go of Sadie long enough to give Gage a quick hand shake and a shoulder clap. Neither of them was the bro-hug type, which was just one of the reasons why Gage really liked Nick.

Nick raised a brow at Colin Farrell, who was happily sniffing each of the throw pillows on the couch. The dog would most likely make himself at home among them once he determined the most comfortable spot. Gage had only known him for a day, but Colin was predictable. His only concerns in life were who was going to scratch his ears, when he was going to eat, and where he was going to sleep.

"I thought you said you were bringing a dog," Nick said. "That's livestock."

Sadie waved a hand dismissively. "You won't even know he's here."

Colin Farrell chose that moment to let out a fart so loud he startled himself and immediately started spinning in a circle, trying to see who had snuck up on him and made such a horrifying noise and smell.

Sadie frowned. "OK, well, *maybe* you will know he's here…but he's a good boy, I swear. He's housebroken and hardly ever barks or jumps up on anyone."

Nick glanced over at Gage for confirmation, one brow raised. Gage shrugged and said, "He's no worse than Grandma Ruthie, and I'm sure you've tolerated her as a houseguest at least once."

"Good point," Nick mumbled.

"When do you leave?" Sadie asked him.

"In about an hour," Nick said, looking uneasy. "Are you both sure you're OK to stay the week? It's not going to be awkward or weird or anything, right?"

Because I've seen your sister naked and had my tongue on pretty much every inch of her body and now she wants to just be friends? Why would that be awkward or weird or anything?

But instead of saying *that*, Gage said, "It's fine."

Sadie nodded and offered her brother a warm smile. "We've got this. Don't worry."

YOU WRECKED ME / Isabel Jordan

He shoved a hand through his hair and huffed out a weary sigh. "It's just that…I mean I know you two can take care of everything around here and I trust you both, but…"

Gage couldn't help but notice Nick's focus was more on him than it was on Sadie. "What? You afraid *I'm* not housebroken or that *I'll* jump up on people?"

Sadie gave her brother a hard look. "But *what*, Nick?"

He looked uncomfortable, but after a long pause, Nick said, "Look, I'm just going to be out there with this. The last time the two of you were together, there was a whole shitload of never-ending drama. And Grace's doctor says that while she's on bed rest, she needs to avoid stress and angst and drama of any kind. She needs to chill. I just want to make sure there won't be any kind of…repeats of last time the two of you were in the same room together."

Drama like the fact that Gage wanted Sadie more than his next breath while she needed space? Drama like the fact that Sadie ran out on Grace's little brother and left him at the alter? *That* kind of drama? He shot Sadie a questioning look that she returned with a tight expression of her own.

Sadie licked her lips. "Nick, that was five years ago. I was young and stupid. I've apologized to Michael and he forgave me. Gage and I…we're fine. There's nothing to worry about."

Nick's eyes narrowed as he regarded his sister. "You're sure? Because you two seem…*close*. Like, a kind of *close*ness that could lead to drama in my house. You're telling me that's *not* the case?"

Dude, Gage wanted to say, if you think we're close now, you

YOU WRECKED ME / Isabel Jordan

should've seen us yesterday! But he kept his mouth shut, turning his eyes to Sadie instead. They had a brief, silent conversation at that point, using nothing more than their facial expressions.

Her: *Should I tell him anything about us??*

Him: *Not my call. He's your brother.*

Her: *She's your cousin! Michael's sister!*

Him: *Brother trumps cousin. I'm not touching this one. Tell him whatever you want.*

Sadie scowled at him before turning back to her brother, squaring her shoulders. "You have nothing to worry about, Nick. There's no...drama here."

Nick looked to Gage for confirmation, and Gage forced a neutral expression and a nod. He'd just have to suck up his feelings and pretend he wasn't already half in love with Sadie, because surely unrequited love was all kinds of dramatic.

Sadie looped her arm through Nick's and started asking questions about what Grace would need through the week as they made their way into the living room. Gage's gaze was immediately drawn down to the subtle sway of her hips as she moved. He got half hard just looking at her.

Yeah. Sure. He could pretend they were just friends all week.

He was sooooooo fucked.

CHAPTER FIFTEEN

Nick had been totally exaggerating about the pregnancy hormones.

Or, at least that's what Sadie *would* have said until about an hour ago. Now? Well, now she knew that maybe her brother hadn't been exaggerating *enough* about Grace's emotional state.

After Nick reluctantly left for work (or rather, after Gage finally got sick of him making excuses for why he *couldn't* leave and shoved him out the door), Sadie, Gage, and Grace had a lovely chat to catch up and figure out everything that needed to be done during the week.

Grace positively glowed with happiness from her place in the bed, and she was the epitome of soon-to-be-mom chic in her fancy silk PJs, propped up on a mountain of throw pillows. Surrounded by baby books with dog-eared pages and with a lengthy to-do checklist at her side, she looked ready to grab parenting by the balls and make it her bitch.

She'd even quickly fallen in love with Colin Farrell, who curled up on the chaise next to Grace's bed and lifted his head occasionally to give her his slobbery, doggy grin and gaze at her adoringly.

They'd laughed and joked around, and Grace had been in high

spirits. For a while, at least.

Looking back, Sadie thought things started to circle the drain when Grace got hungry, which Nick had warned her about.

"Whatever you do, don't let her skip her snacks," he'd said, his tone and expression so grim that Sadie had laughed out loud at him.

"You make her sound like a gremlin, for God's sake, Nicky," she'd replied. "Do I need to make sure not to feed her after midnight, too?"

But she wasn't laughing now.

Grace had gone from smiling and laughing one minute, to near-tears and snappish (like, bite-your-head-off-and-spit-it- across-the-room snappish) in less time than it had taken Sadie to wonder idly if her sister-in-law's head was going to start spinning around like Linda Blair's character in *The Exorcist.*

Grace had asked for French fries from McDonald's for her afternoon snack. Gage had reminded her about her preeclampsia and about how too much salt wasn't good for her or the baby.

And that's when everything went a little wonky.

Sadie had watched it all unfold in a bit of a stupefied daze as Grace railed on Gage about mansplaining and white male privilege and how people without vaginas shouldn't have any say in what a pregnant lady was allowed to eat. When Gage tried to explain that people with medical degrees absolutely *should* be able to advise pregnant ladies with preeclampsia not to eat too much salt, Sadie had wanted to tell him to shut the hell up and maybe duck and cover for safety.

After that, threats were made, pillows were thrown, and Gage finally relented and agreed to get her a small order of fries that she could enjoy along with the fresh fruit salad Nick had made for her.

Then Grace collapsed against the pillows in a fresh fit of tears, apologizing for being so difficult, begging Gage's forgiveness, and wondering what the hell could be wrong with her. Sadie patted her hand and did her best to soothe her without reminding her that it was most likely the watermelon-sized leech in her womb that was currently sucking out her sanity.

Gage had just muttered, "Jesus," and made his way out the door like the room was on fire to go and get Grace her fries. Judging by the look on his face when he left, Sadie imagined Gage had changed his stance on Grace's salt intake and would probably be willing to pour the stuff directly down Grace's gullet by the pound if it kept her from weeping on him again.

Men, Sadie thought, internally scoffing. They never did know what to do with a woman in tears.

When he was gone, Grace pulled a tissue out of the box on her nightstand and dabbed at her eyes. "So, what's going on with you and Gage?"

Sadie blinked at her absolutely calm and cool tone. It was as if the sobbing, hysterical woman from a mere moment ago had fled the building and left a non-pregnant, rational, lawyerly woman in her place. And given the calculating look in her eye, Sadie wasn't sure which Grace she preferred.

"The ride here was uneventful," she said, employing evasive maneuvers. "Boring as hell, but I guess that beats the alternative, right?"

But lawyerly Grace wouldn't be deterred. "That's not what I mean and you know it. There's tension there. I can feel it."

Red alert! Red alert!

Sadie did her best to exude pure innocence as she returned Grace's shrewd stare. "Tension? No, I don't think so. We're getting along fine."

Yesterday we got along, like, multiple-orgasms fine, if you want to know the truth. So, so many lovely orgasms...

Grace narrowed her eyes on Sadie. "Look, I'm pregnant, not blind. I know something is going on. I also know Nick warned you not to stress me out or cause any drama because of my blood pressure."

Geez, how did a woman who was stuck in bed all day riding an emotional roller coaster of pregnancy hormones know so much about what was going in her house?

Sadie's shock must have shown on her face because Grace chuckled and answered her unspoken questions with, "Like I said, I'm pregnant, not deaf, dumb, and blind. And Nick's voice carries like crazy in this house. I heard everything he said to you."

Now Sadie was torn. Grace knew something was going on, but Nick had made her promise not to bring drama into the house. What she had going on with Gage had *all* sorts of drama potential. And Grace was the type of person who would want to help fix all the potential problems and make everyone happy, which would ultimately just lead to more stress. It was a catch-22.

"OK," Sadie began carefully, "I'll admit that there's something going on with me and Gage. It's nothing for you to worry about or get involved in. We're fine. We're both on the same page." *Kind of.* "Neither one of us is going to talk about it with you. Not because we don't want to, but because Nick made us promise not to dump drama on your doorstep and if you go into early labor, my brother will kill me and Gage. Fair enough?"

Grace considered Sadie's words for what felt like an eternity, then pouted and said, "Fair enough. But…you're happy? You're both happy? That's all I need to know and I'll be able to relax."

Sadie felt her cheeks go pink at the thought of just how *happy* Gage had made her recently. Grace's knowing, answering smile only made her blush harder.

"Well," Grace eventually said, sounding smug enough that it made Sadie a little uncomfortable, "I guess we're in for a happy, uneventful, non-stressful week then, aren't we?"

The urge to knock on wood was suddenly damn-near overwhelming, but Sadie gulped and said, "Of course! Everything will be just fine."

Hey, Karma…don't make me regret saying that. Please and thank you.

CHAPTER SIXTEEN

Gage dumped the French fries on the serving tray next to Grace's fruit salad and a bottle of water and set the whole thing on her lap with a grand flourish. "Your snack, m'lady," he quipped in his best British manservant accent. He offered her a deep bow. "Beggin' your pardon for my earlier insolence. Hopin' you'll see it in your heart not to fire me and send me to the work house, m'lady."

She rolled her eyes. "Don't be a dick, Jeeves."

"Such language. You gonna kiss your baby with that mouth?"

Grace pouted. "No one likes you, you know."

Gage sat down on the edge of her bed. "Oh, you know you love me. Always have."

"It's true," she said with a disgusted sigh. "You're pretty OK for a grumpy bastard."

"That's what all the ladies say."

She gave him a shrewd side-eye that set his teeth on edge and said, "Is that what *Sadie* says about you?"

He pointed his index finger at her. "I'm not falling for that. Sadie already told me you're fishing. There will be *no drama* in this house all week. You're just going to have to deal with it."

She groaned and threw her head back against her pillow.

"You're such a killjoy," she muttered. "You aren't going to tell me *anything* about what's going on with you two?"

"I'll tell you everything you need to know."

After a moment of pointed silence, Grace frowned at him and threw a fry at his head. Thankfully his quick reflexes allowed him to catch it before it went into his eye—Grace had great aim for a bedridden pregnant lady—and toss it back onto her tray. He almost laughed at the disgruntled look on her face when the fry missed its mark.

But her expression quickly faded to something else as she continued to watch him. "What?" he finally asked, unnerved.

She shrugged, and her lower lip started to tremble. "It's just...I'm so happy and I want you to be happy, too. You've always been kind of grumpy and sullen, even when we were kids."

Well, if that didn't make him sound like a pathetic humorless fuck he didn't know what would. "Um...I'm sorry?"

"No, no, no," she said, grabbing his hand. "It's just that... you've had so little true happiness in your life. You deserve it, you know."

He was about to make a smart-assed comment, but the way her eyes were filling up with tears made him rethink it. "Oh, God, you're not going to cry again, are you?"

She frowned at him sternly, but then nodded as tears started dripping down her cheeks.

Gage gave her hand a squeeze. "Cry as much or as little as you want, but never about me, OK? I'm fine. I'm...happy."

Or, at least he was starting to realize he *could* be happy. It wasn't an impossibility for him, as he'd once feared. He'd seen glimpses of what happy felt like when he was with Sadie.

Now if only he could convince Sadie to let go and be happy with him…

CHAPTER SEVENTEEN

Sadie made her way to the door, saying a silent prayer to any gods who might be listening that Grace wouldn't wake up before she was able to make her escape.

Colin Farrell lifted his head and watched her ease out the door, but Sadie gave him an "everything's OK" hand wave that he seemed to understand, because he immediately dropped his giant head back down on Grace's thigh with a little huff of pleasure.

When she'd made it to the safety of the hallway, she let out a huge sigh of relief and went to the nursery, where Gage had been working most of the day.

She found him standing in the empty room on a painting drop cloth, roller in one hand and a beer in the other, as he swiped sunny yellow paint on the white wall. He was barefoot, and the way he looked in loose gray sweatpants and a white T-shirt should be illegal. Muscles straining, big, strong hands at work, that face, those intense eyes…it was pornographic, really.

Idly Sadie considered filming him while he worked and uploading it to YouTube just to see how long it would take the video to go viral. And she had no doubt it'd go viral. The demand for video of ridiculously hot guys doing manual labor had to be pretty huge, she thought.

Then he ruined a little of his hot factor by muttering, "Why the hell would anyone want to paint a room the color of Big Bird's ass?"

Sadie chuckled and moved to stand next to him, hands on her hips as she examined the wall color. "I like it. It's…happy. And gender-neutral, which is good since they opted not to find out the baby's sex. It'll work for a boy's room or a girl's room."

"Or a Mexican cantina."

Sadie hip-bumped him. "Such a grumpy skeptic. Just don't tell Grace you don't like the color. You'll make her cry again."

He shuddered. "Noted. I think I've done that enough today."

"Well, in all honesty, how were you supposed to know she had such strong feelings about the possibility of a Wolverine movie reboot that didn't include Hugh Jackman?"

"Right?"

She glanced around while he kept painting, taking note of all he'd gotten done while she'd been stuck in a room with Grace watching *Beaches*. Twice.

He'd picked up Grace's paint order at the hardware store, completely emptied the room that had once been an office, and taped off all the white trim and the room's four windows. Once the painting was done, all they'd need to do was go to the baby superstore and pick up the stuff on Grace's list to stock the room.

"Wow," she said, "you got a shit ton of work done today. I'm really impressed."

He snorted. "Don't be. I would've done pretty much anything

to get out of watching TV with Grace."

Sadie shook her head. "I know, right? If she hadn't dozed off, I'm pretty sure she intended to make me watch *The Notebook*. I mean, I love Grace, but her taste in movies and TV shows is total crap."

"It didn't used to be. I'm going to blame the pregnancy. Again."

"Makes me glad I've been on the pill since I was fifteen."

He froze, roller in mid-air, and gave her a look so potent it damn near melted her clothes off. That's when it occurred to her that the condoms they'd run out of the morning before their cross-country road trip were irrelevant. And if both of them were clean—which, she knew she was and assumed he was, especially given his five-year dry spell—they could've totally have sex without any barriers between them.

If she got her shit together emotionally, she could un-friend-zone him and have sex with him *now* without any barriers between them.

Oh. Holy. Fuck.

He had the same thought. She could see it in his eyes. His brow furrowed a little and he looked like he was doing the math on how long it would take to get them both naked and what surface he should pin her against.

10.5 seconds and against the door, Sadie calculated. She'd always been good at math.

Gage turned to her slowly, eyes dropping to her mouth, and her body swayed toward his of its own volition. It was like his sexiness had its own gravitational pull and she was helpless against it.

But her inner critic, the annoying, judge-y one who always nagged her about doing the *right* thing versus the *fun* thing, reminded her that their timing was, once again, all wrong. When her lips were a heartbeat away from her his, she pulled back regretfully. (Oh, the regret. So, *so* much regret).

"We can't do *that* in the baby's room," she whispered.

His answering smile did things to her—naughty, naughty things—that also shouldn't be done in the baby's room.

"Why are we whispering?" he asked. "The baby isn't here yet and the baby momma is sound asleep."

Because it just feels wrong to be fantasizing about screaming, dirty sex in a nursery while Grace sleeps in the next room, OK?

Even though she was 99% sure she hadn't said that out loud, he smiled as if he'd heard her. And that smile did such naughty, naughty things to her and got even hotter as he leaned toward her again. "You're all flushed," he said, his calm tone completely at odds with the heat and dirty, dirty mischief in his eyes. "Anything I can do to help?"

She couldn't hold back a moan at the thought of what he could do to help her. It took every ounce of strength she had not to lean forward and bite his lower lip, then kiss the crap out of him. He'd taste so good, she knew. Like beer and heat and multiple screaming orgasms.

Sadie licked her lips and almost moaned again when his eyes tracked the motion. "You know," she began carefully, "I've heard that *some* friends *sometimes* get naked with each other."

He raised a brow. "Is that so?"

She nodded. "Yep. Naked friends. It's a thing."

He held her gaze as he set the paint roller back in the tray and put his beer down next to it. She was suddenly way too aware of her breathing and her skin felt too tight. If he didn't touch her soon, she might have a stroke.

"Well," he said, "being naked friends would certainly give me *some* of the things I want from you."

"Some?"

"Hmmm."

Then her breathing all but stopped as he reached out and tucked a strand of hair that had worked its way out of her messy bun behind her ear and swiped his thumb gently over her lower lip. He leaned in and whispered in her ear, "But it wouldn't give me everything. And I want *everything* with you. I'm greedy that way."

Yes! Everything, her heart shouted. Take it! It's all yours!

And the fact that her heart was just *so* eager to throw itself at him was doused her libido with ice water.

When she didn't say anything, he pulled back and shoved his hands through his hair. "I'll take your silence as confirmation that the *just-friends* plan is still in effect."

She swallowed hard. It wasn't fair to have sex with him, knowing she wasn't ready to commit fully just yet. It'd feel too much like using him, and he deserved better. "I'm sorry. I still need a little time, I guess."

"Don't be sorry."

YOU WRECKED ME / Isabel Jordan

And with that, he picked up the roller and handed it to her. "Help me get this done and I'll buy you a pizza with extra peppers and sausage, just the way you like it. I'll even throw in a bottle of wine, as long as you're sure you can keep your hands to yourself after you've had a few glasses. Friend."

His eyes sparkled with humor as she frowned at him. "I can if you can," she challenged.

"I guess we'll just have to see, won't we?"

CHAPTER EIGHTEEN

Sadie woke up out of a dead sleep and screeched bloody murder when something hot and wet slid into her ear. Visions of the worm Khan put in Chekhov's ear in *The Wrath of Khan* danced through her sleepy brain as she scrubbed furiously at her head and rolled off Gage's prone form onto the floor.

Blinking furiously to clear the sleep from her eyes, she glanced over at Gage, who was still sound asleep right next to her. Wait…why was he on the floor? Wait…why had she been on top of him on the floor?

Suddenly a giant furry head appeared above her, blocking her view of Gage and the obnoxiously bright yellow wall beyond him. Colin Farrell wagged his tail lazily and licked her from chin to forehead with one swipe of his hot, wet tongue.

"Ugh," Sadie groaned, wiping the dog spit off her face with her forearm. "Well, that explains what woke me up."

She supposed she should just be grateful it had been Colin Farrell's tongue and not a Ceti eel that had plundered her ear canal. (And no, she was not at all ashamed to know the name of the ear worm from *The Wrath of Khan*. It was a highly underrated film in her opinion, and she'd stand firmly by her nerd knowledge until the end of times.)

But that was about all she was grateful for at the moment, she realized as her head pounded and her mouth tasted like she'd brushed her teeth with a dead possum. And not even a clean, fresh roadkill possum. Her mouth tasted like a dead possum that'd been pulled out of a dumpster behind the food court at the mall. After three days of ninety-degree weather.

Blech.

Sitting up with another groan, she dropped her forehead to her palm and silently cursed the two bottles of wine she'd finished off with minimal help from Gage the previous night. He'd been smart and stuck mostly with beer, so he probably didn't feel like his brain was going to liquefy and start dripping out his ears at any moment.

Lucky bastard.

Colin Farrell nudged her with his nose and gave a little whine. "You gotta go out, handsome boy?" she asked.

He barked his excitement and Sadie winced as the noise punched through her skull and poked her brain. With Herculean effort, she hoisted herself up off the floor, groaning as the room spun a little, and wobbled her way down the stairs to let Colin Farrell out. He trotted happily into Nick and Grace's fenced-in backyard, did his business, then high-tailed it back towards the house before flopping over on the porch in the sun. He glanced back at her and offered her two lazy tail wags, which she took as her dismissal.

"Well, OK then," she told him, chuckling. "Enjoy your morning."

Even though all she wanted to do was mainline a pot of coffee and sit in complete silence and darkness for the rest of the day, Sadie decided she better check on Grace. *Stupid adult responsibilities.* So, she trudged up the steps and peeked into Grace's room.

Grace was wide awake, sitting with her back against her padded headboard, wearing her fancy PJs and reading glasses, looking over something on her computer. She looked alert and so bright and shiny that Sadie instinctively covered her eyes.

Grace took one look at her and burst out laughing. When her laughter died down, she said, "Well, good morning, sunshine. After what I heard last night, I'm surprised to see you conscious this early in the morning."

The rusty wheels in Sadie's brain started spinning as she tried to think of anything Grace might have heard the previous night. *Oh crap, had Gage finally agreed to be naked friends last night and she was too drunk to remember it? That'd suck!*

No, Sadie realized after a moment. They hadn't had sex last night. Just pizza and wine. And more wine. And more wine. And…

"Oh, God," Sadie said on a groan as memories of the previous night started to flash through her foggy brain, "did I *sing* last night?"

Grace's grin was pure evil. "Yep. Sounded like you and Gage had one hell of a festive painting party. It was awesome."

If memory served, it'd been her idea to play some music while painting. And somewhere after her fourth—or was it her fifth?—glass of wine, it'd seemed like a fabulous idea to sing along.

Now, Sadie knew she wasn't devoid of talent. There were some things she was really good at. Hell, she kicked ass at Jeopardy, could recite lines from pretty much any '80s movie, and thanks to an assignment that put her in Marine boot camp for a week, she knew she was above average on an obstacle course. But singing? Not her thing. She couldn't carry a tune in a bucket.

What song had she tried—and failed—to tackle? Oh, shit, she hoped there hadn't been too many high notes.

Grace's smile grew, reminding Sadie of the Grinch moments after he'd devised his plan to steal Christmas. That's when Sadie remembered.

"Fuuucccckkkk...tell me I didn't sing that."

"Yep," Grace said, popping the "p". "*Take On Me* by A-Ha. But only after you gave *Barracuda* a go."

"Fuuucccckkkk."

Grace laughed again, then said, "Don't worry about it. It was awesome."

Sadie cocked her head to the side like a confused terrier. "My voice? It couldn't possibly have been."

"Oh, no, your voice was terrible," Grace said with a chuckle. "What was awesome was Gage."

Sadie didn't remember Gage singing. But if that bastard could sing, she was going to be pissed. It was truly unfair for someone *that* hot and *that* smart to be super-talented, too. She sniffed indignantly. "Well, even if he was better than me, I'm guessing his song choice was less ambitious. The degree of difficulty should count for something."

"Oh, Lord, no, Gage didn't sing." Grace seemed amused by the mere idea of Gage bursting into song. "What was awesome was the way he laughed and joked around with you while *you* were singing."

Yeah, now that Grace mentioned it, Sadie remembered that, too. They'd talked and laughed and talked some more. It'd been…everything.

The physical chemistry she had with Gage was one thing. But the way she could make him laugh? The way he made her feel like the only woman in the room—in the world? The way they connected on a bone-deep level? It was crazy. And overwhelming. And exactly what she'd always been searching for in her life. A place where she belonged with people who understood her and only wanted her to be exactly who she was.

Gage felt like…home. The home she'd never had.

And after everything she'd been through, she was too messed up emotionally to let go and trust that feeling, to take what Gage was offering her. Everything she'd ever wanted was within in her grasp and she was too much of a chicken to take it. What kind of sick fucking irony was *that*?

"Look," Grace said, lowering her voice a bit, "I understand that you're scared and reluctant to make any commitments at this point. But don't…close yourself off to any possibilities, either, OK? Don't be afraid to open your heart."

Being afraid to open her heart had never been Sadie's problem. If anything, her heart had always been *too* open. She thought she'd moved beyond that in the past five years. But here she was, ready to hand Gage her heart. Maybe she hadn't grown up as much as she thought she had since she first met Gage.

So, she supposed, since her heart wasn't entirely trustworthy at this point, all she could do was wait this thing out. If she was meant to be with Gage, he'd wait for her to be ready for a relationship. That was all there was to it. Time would tell.

Fuck time, her heart and body pleaded. *Take him now!*

Sadie fought back a groan and rubbed her pounding temples. These little internal heart-and-body-versus-brain battles needed to stop. It was exhausting and her brain was way too worn out—and wine-logged to keep arguing logically.

"I hear what you're saying, Grace," Sadie eventually said, "but I meant what I told Nicky. There won't be any drama this week. So no more talk about me and Gage, OK? We're just…friends."

Grace's gaze dropped to Sadie's chest and she smirked in a way that made Sadie wonder if facial expressions were hereditary, because she was *sure* she'd seen Gage give her that very same smirk a time or two. Or ten.

"Oh, I can tell," Grace said, sarcasm positively dripping from her tongue. "*Totally* just friends."

Sadie glanced down at her chest and saw two perfect yellow handprints—*large* handprints—on her white shirt, right over her boobs.

Her alcohol-soaked memory supplied her with a quick flash of Gage cupping her breasts with his paint-covered hands as a joke. He'd laughed it off. But there'd been nothing *just friends* about how much she'd wanted him in that moment. Or in this moment, for that matter.

"Balls," Sadie muttered.

Listening to logic instead of her body and heart was *not* going to be easy, especially when her body and heart made *such* a compelling case.

"Morning."

Sadie spun around at Gage's grumbly, sleepy voice, and damn it, he looked like a freaking walking, talking wet dream as he leaned a shoulder against Grace's doorjamb and ran a hand through his already-mussed hair.

His eyes dropped to the handprints on her chest and his grin was all kinds of sinful, not at all repentant. Her own eyes dropped and she clapped a hand over her mouth to stifle a horrified gasp when she found a perfect yellow handprint—a small one, exactly the size of her own hand—on his crotch.

Sadie whipped her head around to find Grace giving the two of them a shit-eating grin. "Gage," she asked, sounding like she was fighting off a chuckle, "did you take advantage of my little sister-in-law last night?"

He glanced down at the handprint on his crotch and shrugged. "Looks like maybe she took advantage of me first."

"Balls," Sadie hissed again, face-palming.

"Oh, relax," Grace said, finally letting her laugh go. "Shit happens when alcohol is involved. You guys can stick with the whole *just friends* thing. I don't care."

Thank God.

But Sadie's relief was short-lived as Grace's gaze dropped to Sadie's chest again and her expression crumbled. Tears filled her eyes

120

as she asked, voice wobbly, "Is that the new color I picked for the baby's room?"

"Yes," Gage answered, eyeing his cousin like a tripwire he had to step over to avoid being blown sky-high. "Why?"

Her lower lip quivered for a moment as she wailed, "It looks like Big Bird's ass!"

Gage shot Sadie an I-told-you-so look before shaking his head and muttering, "Balls."

CHAPTER NINETEEN

Gage had a lengthy—*way* too lengthy for his liking—conversation with Robbie, the kid at the Home Depot paint counter who had been working with Grace trying to pick the right color for the nursery for the past six months.

"Take the Big Bird paint back to Robbie, explain that it was for me, and he'll be happy to help you get the right color," Grace had said. "He's super-helpful."

But, oddly enough, as soon as Gage had mentioned Grace by name, the *super-helpful* Robbie looked ready to have a nervous breakdown. Gage had to promise the kid that Grace was home on bedrest and wouldn't be coming in just to keep him from crying.

"I tried to tell her the color would be really bright, maybe too bright for the baby's room," Robbie said once he was sure Grace wasn't hiding behind a stack of painting tarps, ready to jump out and ambush him. "But she said I was wrong and started talking about mansplaining and *the man* keeping her down and some legal stuff I didn't really follow. Then when I called my manager, she started apologizing and crying, so we just said she could go and that we'd mix the paint up for Mr. O'Connor to pick up later. I'm pretty sure we didn't even charge her for it, man. I mean, that yellow was the seventh paint we'd sold her that turned out to be wrong for some reason. At this point, we just all want it to be over."

Gage could relate.

Mr. O'Connor had failed to mention the six other times that nursery had been painted, letting Gage go in completely blind. He'd be sure to thank *Mr. O'Connor* for that when the fucker got home.

But eventually, with Robbie's help, Gage had settled on a soft, warm cream color he was fairly sure Grace would love once the pregnancy hormones stopped holding her hostage. So, with paint in hand—or, in the back of his SUV, at least—he made his way through the drive-through at the deli to pick up Grace's chicken salad sandwich and kettle chips.

He'd given up arguing with her about her salt intake. She was only a week shy of her due date at this point, and the stress of not getting what she wanted seemed to take more of a toll on her than the salt ever would. So if he never fought another battle with his cousin over sodium, he could die happy.

His phone rang as he thanked the drive-through employee for Grace's food, and he smiled when he saw Sadie's name pop up on the screen.

Damn, he was really screwed if just the sight of a woman's name on a screen could make him happy.

"Her majesty has changed her lunch order," Sadie said when he answered, sounding frazzled. "She'd now like chicken tacos."

He sighed, repressing a growl. The ever-changing food orders were getting old. "I just got her the chicken salad. She's going to have to make do with that. I'll get her tacos for dinner or something."

There was a loaded pause on Sadie's end before she said, "Gage, I don't think you heard me." Her tone was low, a little frantic, and deadly serious. "The woman who just made me watch *The Notebook* for the second time today said she wants chicken tacos. I've been walking on egg shells all damn day because apparently, anything I say can and will be used against me in a fit of hormonal tears. She's like twenty different people in one body. I feel like I've spent my day trying to break up a gang fight, Gage, but the gang members are bears and sharks, and the bears and sharks have switchblades and ADHD and they're fighting on an active volcano that's ready to erupt at any minute. And you're asking me to go back into the gang fight, put my body between the armed sharks and bears, and tell her that there aren't going to be any chicken tacos. Do you understand what I'm saying?"

She'd said it all in one breath. That was pretty damn impressive. And hilarious.

God, this woman…

Well, he figured laughing would be inappropriate, so instead, he calmly said, "So, you're saying I should pick up some chicken tacos?"

He could imagine her pinching the bridge of her nose like she always did when she was frustrated and it just made him want to rush back and kiss the hell out of her because she was ridiculously cute when she was frustrated.

"Yes, Gage, *that* is what I'm saying."

"OK." Then, because he was an asshole, he added, "Why

didn't you just say so in the first place?"

Another pause on her end before he heard her hold the phone away from her mouth and yell, "Hey, Grace! Gage says he's never watched *Fried Green Tomatoes*. You have that one, don't you?"

He didn't hear Grace's words, but the enthusiasm in her reply was clear. It seemed he'd be watching *Fried Green Tomatoes* when he returned with the chicken tacos. Fuuuucccckkkk.

Well played, Sadie. Well played.

"Take that," she said, her voice full of smugness. Too bad for her that the only thing he found cuter than frustrated Sadie was smug Sadie.

"Oh, that was bad," he said silkily. "You need to be *punished* for that."

Her intake of breath was sharp enough to let Gage know her mind immediately flew into the gutter at his mention of punishment, just like he knew it would. Another thing he loved about Sadie? While she might look like an angel, she was anything *but* angelic when it came to sex.

And while she was chronically commitment-shy, she'd never denied their chemistry. Her "naked friends" suggestion proved that. It had taken every ounce of will power Gage had to refuse that suggestion.

But, true to form, she recovered quickly, firing back, "No one likes a tease, Gage Montgomery."

And before he could even snort out a laugh, she'd hung up on him.

Sadie O'Connor was a little neurotic, a total commitment-phobe, and expected him to talk way more than he felt was necessary. She was also gorgeous, funny, wicked smart, and secretly a little dark and twisted. Not to mention she was sexy as hell.

I'm gonna marry that girl.

He knew it without question. He was going to do whatever it took to convince her to be his forever.

Fuck all this just friends *shit.*

CHAPTER TWENTY

"Look, I helped repaint the baby's room *again*, watched fucking *Fried Green Tomatoes*, filled out all your baby gift thank you notes from the shower and dropped them off at the post office. I've done enough. There's no way I'm going to some stupid suburban dinner party on your behalf to deliver a damn fruit tart," Sadie said.

Or, at least, that's what Sadie said in her *head*. She'd *started* to say it out loud, but as soon as Grace's eyes misted over with tears and her lower lip started to wobble, Sadie had folded like a cheap card table.

Now, like an idiot, she stood on the front porch of Grace and Nick's neighbor's house, stupid tart in hand, ringing the doorbell and expecting to be let in to socialize with complete strangers just because a crazy pregnant lady had volunteered to bring a fruit tart before she went on bedrest and felt *certain* the entire party would fail if these people were forced to go without fruit for the night.

Sadie glanced over at Gage and grinned at the sour expression on his face. Somehow knowing he hated this more than she did made it all more tolerable. "Hey, it could be worse," she said.

"How? How could this be worse?"

"Well, you didn't have to make the fruit tart—you're welcome, by the way—and Grace's plan for the evening was to watch *Steel*

Magnolias."

"And why do we both have to be here again?" he asked. "Couldn't we just drop the fruit tart here and run away?"

That idea wasn't half bad.

But it would never work, she realized. Grace would know if they blew off her request to meet the neighbors and spend time with them on her behalf. "Well, if we're keeping with the 'give Grace whatever she wants' theme we've been sticking with so far, she was pretty adamant that she wanted us here."

He glanced down at her, a little frown line knitting his brow. "Why do you think she wanted us both here so bad? Doesn't it seem weird to you?"

She frowned. "Yeah, a little, I guess. But no more so than her newfound love of awful movies."

"True. I just have a weird feeling about this. The last time she insisted I show up to some social thing she tried to—"

Whatever Gage was going to say next was lost when the door swung open and a woman in a skin-tight red mini dress stood before them, eyeing Gage like he was a thick, juicy steak on a plate and she'd been on a month-long fast.

The woman licked her ruby-painted, plump lower lip and fluttered her obviously false eyelashes at him. "You must be Gage, Grace's cousin, the *doctor.* I've been after her for *years* to get you over here to one of these neighborhood parties."

The emphasis she put on Gage's name and the word *doctor* made Sadie feel like they'd just stumbled into a porno. If anyone demanded they put their car keys in a bowl to swap partners like in *The Ice Storm*, Sadie was going to be *pissed*.

Gage glanced down at Sadie, one brow raised, and finished his earlier statement with a muttered, indignant, "—fix me up."

Sadie's eyes flew back to the woman who'd just introduced herself as Libby and was ushering them into a house nearly identical to Grace and Nick's, only this one had a more formal decorating style that made Sadie glad she'd opted to wear a stylish yellow sundress instead of the jeans and T-shirt she'd originally considered.

But even though she'd dressed up and put a bit of extra time into smoothing her hair and applying makeup—which she rarely ever wore these days and barely remembered how to do—she was still woefully underdressed next to the gorgeous Libby.

Libby was tall, at least 6'0" in her strappy heels, because she towered over Sadie, who wasn't exactly petite at 5'8" in her pretty ballet flats. With her porcelain skin, white-blonde hair, and expertly applied makeup, Libby was practically Sadie's polar opposite. She looked to be about Gage's age, maybe a little older, and polished in a way that Sadie couldn't imagine ever being able to pull off.

Was *this* the kind of woman Grace thought Gage should end up with?

As they made small talk—and Libby took every opportunity to touch Gage—something Sadie wasn't used to feeling bubbled up inside her. It was a kind of simmering rage and jealousy that burned through her veins every time Gage said something that made Libby flip her pretty blonde hair and smile up at him like he was the funniest man in the world.

What made it worse was that Libby was actually a very nice woman. Sure, she was flirting shamelessly with Gage, but she also made a point to include Sadie in the conversation and kept offering her open, guileless smiles that made Sadie feel like a total bitch for wanting to rip Libby's manicured hands off Gage's body every time she touched him.

Gage was hers, damn it! How dare this woman flirt with him right in front of her?

But he's not really yours, her brain reminded her. He could have been, could be, but she'd told him she needed time, needed space, to sort her shit out. If he wanted to go out with—or do anything *else* with—Libby, he could and it would be Sadie's fault for not speaking up and making her feelings for Gage known sooner.

So, Sadie just gritted her teeth while Libby introduced them to everyone else in attendance—she'd never remember everyone's names, but there was a chiropractor, a vet, a history professor at the local community college, a construction foreman, and a mechanic.

Then Libby introduced them to the homeowners, the Michaelsons. Both of them were family law attorneys. Apparently Libby was a Michaelson, too. Sadie hadn't been paying enough attention to the introductions to pick up on how she fit into the family, though.

She'd been too distracted by the sight of Libby's hand wrapped around Gage's arm, like he was her date for the evening.

Or her prey.

And now, twenty minutes after Libby had pawned her off on the chiropractor, who was single, Libby had told her encouragingly, Sadie sat on the Michaelson's tasteful divan, sucking down a much-needed glass of chardonnay, trying not to wonder if Gage was actually enjoying all the attention Libby was throwing his way.

He seemed to be carrying on a fairly decent conversation with her, which delighted and annoyed Sadie in equal measure. On the one hand, yay Gage for making polite small talk with a stranger. She knew that wasn't easy for him, and she'd like to think that—on some level— she'd helped him get to the point where he could do that. But on the other hand...

Did the stranger with whom he was making polite conversation have to be so freakin' beautiful and so obviously interested in getting into his pants?

"You know, if you're not careful, you're going to break that glass."

The voice startled Sadie and she almost sloshed chardonnay all over herself. Then she remembered she was sitting next to a man who'd probably been trying to talk to her for the past...oh, who knows...twenty-eight hours or so. At least that's how long it felt like.

She met his kind brown eyes and offered him what she hoped was an apologetic smile. "I'm so sorry, I didn't quite catch that. What were you saying, Ted?"

He shook his head, looking like he might be fighting off a smile of his own. "It's Tom."

Mental face palm. "Oh, Tom...I'm so sorry. I swear I'm not

usually this rude. I'm having an off night, I guess."

Tom jerked his chin in Gage's direction. "Fight with your boyfriend?"

"No, no. He's not my boyfriend. He's just...well, it's complicated."

"Doesn't look too complicated from where I'm sitting. You've been watching him for most of the past hour, and when you aren't looking, he's watching you. The only thing that seems complicated is why you're talking to me and he's talking to Libby when you clearly only want to be talking to each other."

He's been looking at me? Really? Her inner teenager squealed with glee until her inner adult gave the little twit a much-needed smackdown. Sadie cleared her throat. "Well, let's just say we haven't been on the same page lately. We want different things."

Tom rolled his eyes, but gave her a good-natured smile. "Ah, to be young and stupid again. To not realize that all the petty drama doesn't mean anything at all in the long run. Trust me: if there's love, you can work out the rest, whatever it is."

She frowned at him. "I thought you said you were a chiropractor, Tom, not a shrink. What's with the Dr. Phil routine?"

He chuckled. "No Dr. Phil routine. Just a guy with a broken marriage behind him. And if my ex had ever looked at me the way you two are looking at each other now? Well...let's just say she wouldn't be my *ex*, if you know what I mean."

That's when Sadie noticed that Tom was a good-looking guy. Clean-cut, blond, guy-next-door handsome. And he was obviously a nice guy, since he wasn't even mad at her for ignoring him for the past hour. He reminded her of Michael, actually. Sweet and totally non-threatening. The kind of guy who would never challenge her on anything. A *safe* guy.

Tom was exactly the kind of guy she would've clung to in her past. He was everything she used to want...and everything she *didn't* want now.

God help her, she wanted to be challenged. She wanted a man who was fierce and loyal and who made her think and feel all the emotions, not just the safe ones.

She wanted Gage. Now and for as long as he'd have her, she wanted Gage. Screw her past! Screw her fear of getting too attached and losing herself. She was more...*herself* with Gage than she'd ever been with anyone else in her life.

And what was he doing while she was having her big epiphany?

He was talking to a gorgeous woman who was hanging on his every word and looking up at him like he was the last Krispy Kreme in the box.

Balls.

Tom offered her his hand. "Come on. Let's hit the bar again. We'll do a shot of something ridiculously strong, and maybe that'll give you the courage to go rescue your man from Libby."

She smiled at him and let him help her up. "For what it's worth, Tom, I think your ex is missing out."

CHAPTER TWENTY-ONE

Gage watched Sadie take that douchebag's hand—what was his name again? Ted? Tim?—and head to the bar. The sweet smile she gave the other man made him want to hit something. Or someone. Yeah, definitely someone. Someone named Ted or Tim or whatever would be his first choice.

Not that Ted or Tim or whatever had done anything to Gage. He seemed like an OK guy. Chiropractor, if he remembered correctly. What really bothered Gage about the guy was how much he reminded him of his cousin, Michael.

The guy Sadie had been about to marry.

Maybe Sadie had made her choice and decided she did want a relationship, just not with him. Maybe she wanted a nice, friendly guy like Ted or Tim or whatever. A guy who didn't get stress hives because he was forced to talk to strangers at a fucking dinner party. Could he really blame her for that?

Libby grabbed his forearm, forcing his attention back to her. "You're staring and gritting your teeth again," she said, giving him a sassy grin. "You look like a psychopath when you do that. A ridiculously hot psychopath, but a psychopath nonetheless."

He sighed. He was being a rude jackass to Libby, and she didn't deserve it. "Sorry, Libby. What were you saying?"

She rolled her eyes. "I was telling you where to look for real estate around here, and since I'm the number one realtor in the city, you really *should* have been listening. Instead, you're staring longingly at the girl you want to be with, and menacingly at the guy she *is* with. What I don't understand is why you don't just go over there and tell her how you feel."

"I've already told her how I feel. It's...complicated."

Libby laughed and flipped her hair over one shoulder. "Of course it is! Anything worth having is always a giant fucking mess. The messy stuff is what makes life fun."

"Let's talk about something else," he suggested. "Why don't you give me your business card and let me know when I can stop by your office to talk about real estate, because I wasn't kidding earlier when I said I was considering moving to the area once Grace has her baby."

And just like that, Libby switched from fun, flirty party girl into a tough, smart, sales professional. Or, at least that's what her expression did. The fact that she pulled the business card out of her cleavage hurt her professional demeanor just a smidge.

But before he could take the card from her, Sadie appeared out of nowhere between them, hands on hips, facing off with Libby.

"Look," she began, sounding more pissed off than Gage had ever heard her sound, "I don't want to be a bitch because you've been really nice to me, and I don't want to make a horrible scene in front of all of Grace and Nick's friends, but I've been watching you flirt with

Gage all night, and I can't take it anymore."

Was she...jealous? Of Libby? Gage's dick perked up. Wow. Sadie was always gorgeous, but jealous Sadie? Jealous Sadie was all kinds of fucking *hot*.

Libby held her hands up in surrender. "Oh, honey, there's nothing—"

But apparently Sadie wasn't in the mood to hear what Libby had to say, because she cut her off with, "No, it's OK, because this is partly my fault. I didn't say anything when we first got here, but Gage—" she paused, flinging her hand back towards him, "—is with me. Well, he's not *technically* with me, because when I had my chance to be his, I back-pedaled. But I *am* his. I've been his for a while now; I was just too stupid and scared to admit it. So, I'm hoping he's willing to be mine, too, and you standing there looking so perfect and flirting with him isn't helping my cause any, so I'd like you to stop."

Libby's gaze shifted down to where Sadie's hand had made contact with Gage, and her smile started with nothing more than a twitch of her lower lip, but slowly grew until she was grinning outright.

After a moment of dead silence, Sadie said quietly, "My hand is on his crotch, isn't it?"

Gage glanced down. Yep. Her hand was indeed on his crotch.

Libby let out what could only be described as a cackle. "Honey, I think you and I are going to be *great* friends."

Sadie winced visibly, then pulled her hand back and turned to face Gage. "I just made a complete ass out of myself, didn't I?"

He did his best to rein in his smile. "Yep. Pretty much."

"She wasn't really flirting with you, was she?"

Libby snorted. "I sure as hell was! In the beginning, at least. But he told me right away that he was yours, honey, and I don't poach, so you don't have anything to worry about."

Sadie's lower lip trembled and her eyes got misty. "You told her you were mine?"

He reached out and ran his thumb over that wobbly lower lip of hers. "I've been yours for five years. Are you saying you're ready to be mine?"

She nodded slowly, whispered, "Yes."

"About fucking time."

And with that, he did what he'd been waiting to do for hours—years, really, he supposed. Right there, in front of all of his cousin's friends, he cupped the back of her neck, dragged her into him, and kissed the crap out of her.

When they broke the kiss, Sadie staggered back a step, looking a little dazed and a lot happy. Her smile was nothing short of breathtaking.

If they were in a rom-com, everyone in the room would clap for them at that point. But, since they weren't, they didn't get much more than a couple of curious stares before everyone went back to their own conversations.

"Well, that was nice, huh?" Ted or Tim or whatever said to Libby.

Libby sighed. "Would've been nicer had it been me, but…yeah. I guess that was pretty OK, too."

"Wanna hit the bar with me?"

Libby turned and seemed to see him—really see him—for the first time. "Yes, yes, I would," she said, taking the guy's proffered arm. "Say, I can't remember…do you rent or own your condo?"

His brow furrowed. "Rent."

"Oh, stick with me, honey. I got you."

All's well that ends well, Gage thought, watching Ted or Tim or whatever lead Libby away in search of alcohol.

But that and pretty much all other thoughts he'd ever had in his life fled as Sadie leaned up and whispered in his ear, "I want to fuck you until we can't move. Until we're both completely satisfied and totally spent."

Gage groaned and tugged her toward the door. "About fucking time."

CHAPTER TWENTY-TWO

Non-public places they could get to quickly were in short supply.

The house they were both staying in had a nosy pregnant lady who'd probably be listening to every sound they made and a dog who'd most likely stare at them while they were fucking. That wouldn't do. They were in the middle of the suburbs, so hotels were also in short supply.

There was really only one option that made sense to Sadie.

"Your car," Sadie murmured against his mouth.

She supposed she'd have to take his grunt as an affirmative.

They kissed all the way out of the Michaelsons' house and down their driveway. Sadie reveled in the scrape of his five-o'clock shadow against her jawline, the feel of his mouth against hers, the heat that poured off him.

She felt drunk, even though she'd only had a little alcohol. That was the effect Gage had on her. And she wanted more.

She wanted everything.

Without breaking their hold on each other, they fumbled their way to Gage's car, which was parked on Grace's circular driveway. Sadie hoped Grace was asleep, because if she wasn't, if she happened to be looking out her bedroom window, she was likely to see more than she bargained for.

Still kissing her, Gage wrestled the SUV's back door open. "Are you sure about this?" he asked, then nipped at her lower lip.

Sadie slid into the backseat and growled at him. "Shut up and take off your pants."

"Yes, ma'am," he said, scooting in behind her.

She raised her butt off the seat to yank off her underwear and watched, mesmerized as his nimble fingers undid his fly.

Sadie did some quick mental math about what position might work best for them in the limited space they had, and when her calculations were complete, she inched over on the seat, flipped her skirt up, and got on her hands and knees, which put her ass right in his face.

His answering groan was hot enough that she was pretty sure she could come with that sound alone.

But fortunately, she wouldn't have to find out, because he immediately slid two fingers into her, masterfully hitting the spot—the *perfect* spot—where she needed him the most. She was going to come embarrassingly fast, she realized, but had a hard time caring at the moment.

"Jesus," he muttered, pumping his fingers in and out of her, "You're so wet. So ready."

And she was. Totally, *totally* ready. But it was hard to say anything when you were face-down on a buttery-soft, leather car seat with your ass in the air, about two seconds away from orgasm.

So, she kept her mouth shut and pushed back against his fingers, letting her body do all the talking for her.

Sadie was about to come—so, *so* close—when his hand suddenly stopped moving. Muscles quivering, half a heartbeat away from death by orgasm—or lack thereof, as the case may be—she let out a half-moan/half-wail of frustration. "Don't you dare stop."

"I need to see you," he said in that jagged-glass voice of his. "I need to be in you when you come."

And with that, he reached under her, grabbed her hips, and flipped her over so that her back was on the seat. She tried to do the math on how he'd accomplished *that* in their confined space, but lost all ability to reason when she met his gaze and saw that while he was breathing heavily and his voice sounded strangled, his expression had softened as he gazed down at her.

There was so much tenderness in that expression that her eyes misted over.

"Yes?" he asked one final time. "You're sure?"

There were so few things Sadie was sure of in life. But this…she was sure of this. Of him. She nodded.

"Then hold on."

And then he was easing into her, inch by glorious inch, and all the things she wasn't sure of in life suddenly weren't so important.

***

Gage was pretty sure he was dead. He'd died and gone to heaven. That was really the only explanation for what he was feeling.

He'd thought they'd never be able to top their first time

together, but now, even in the cramped back seat of his car with his legs practically folded the wrong way behind him and her head dangerously close to banging into the door with every thrust, he knew he'd been wrong.

This was as good it was ever going to get. The best it could ever possibly be. And he never wanted to stop. Not now, not tomorrow, not *ever.*

But they couldn't keep doing this forever if she had a concussion, so he left one hand on her hip and slid the other one behind her head so that he could move without hurting her.

Sadie clutched at his hips and locked her ankles behind his knees. "More. Harder."

He didn't need to be told twice.

He started moving, harder and faster, flexing his hips over and over, driving into her until she bit down on her lower lip and moaned. Her eyes were a little hazy with need, but held so much affection for him that he couldn't have looked away, not even if he'd wanted to.

"You're so fucking beautiful," he murmured.

She smiled, reaching up to hook a hand behind his head and yank his mouth down to hers. He kissed her until neither of them could breathe.

When she shifted her hands from his hips up to cup her own breasts, lightly stroking her fingers over her nipples, Gage knew he couldn't last much longer. With a groan, he slid a hand between them and circled his finger over her clit. "Christ, I need you to come first. Can you do that for me?"

"I'm so close," she rasped.

That was all the encouragement he needed to pick up the pace. He moved his hand back to her hip and tightened his other hand in her hair as he slammed into her over and over again, making sure his pelvic bone hit her clit in time with every thrust.

The whimper that erupted from her throat was torture and the best reward he'd ever been given all at the same time. "Come now," he growled through his clenched teeth.

Her hands moved up to rake through his hair, her short nails scraping along his scalp.

"Oh, God, yes!" she cried out.

And with that, her legs trembled and her body tightened around him, milking him relentlessly as her orgasm ripped through her. Holding back was no longer an option for him. One, two, three more thrusts and he followed her right over the edge, muscles straining as the most intense orgasm he'd ever had took control of his body.

Gage really didn't want to crush her, but was pretty sure he might be paralyzed and dehydrated, because he collapsed on her against his will. He buried his face in her soft, sweet-smelling hair and whispered her name.

"Wow," she said on a gusty breath.

Pretty much, he thought.

His pants were still on, her dress was hiked up to her stomach, and they'd just fucked in the back seat of his car like a couple of stupid, horny teenagers.

And he wanted to do it again.

Peace wasn't something he'd had much of in his life, but that's exactly what he felt when he was with her. At peace. Content.

Totally ass-over-elbow in love.

How much would it freak her out if he told her he loved her?

Probably a whole helluva lot, dumbass, he told himself.

Gage raised his head and stared down at her. Her eyes were heavy-lidded, and her mascara was a smudged mess. Her hair was a disaster. And the smile on her kiss-swollen lips was angelic.

He shook his head. "I don't think I'll ever get used to how beautiful you are."

The wattage on that smile amped up considerably as it slipped from angelic to wicked. "Are you just trying to sweet- talk me into round two?"

His dick perked right back up at that, apparently more than willing to go for round two. "Is it working?"

Sadie pulled her knees up around his hips, drawing him in deeper. "Yes."

Well, all right then. Round two it is.

But then Gage's phone started blaring at an unreasonable volume, completely ruining the moment.

Sadie laugh-snorted. "Is that 'God Save the Queen'?"

He groaned, reaching into his pocket to pull the phone out. "That's my ringtone for Grace. Her Highness probably wants me to repaint the nursery again."

"Or buy more Chunky Monkey," Sadie suggested.

"Or watch another soul-sucking chick flick," he muttered.

YOU WRECKED ME / Isabel Jordan

But what he saw on the phone had him wishing she really did want a new paint color, more ice cream, or a re-watch of *Beaches*. He held the screen up so Sadie could see.

Her eyes widened. "912," she whispered. *More important than 911.* "Shit."

CHAPTER TWENTY-THREE

Grace was surprisingly calm for a woman who was in labor and had been certifiably crazy all week.

Sadie hung up the phone and grabbed Grace's hospital bag as Gage lifted her out of the bed and made his way down the stairs. "Ambulance is on the way," she told them. "Five minutes out."

"I can walk," Grace protested.

"And have a contraction while you're on the steps and possibly fall down?" Gage asked, incredulous. "Fuck, no. Nick would kill me."

"He's right," Sadie assured her. "Nick would carry you if he was here."

Grace rolled her eyes. "He would've panicked and called 911 at the first twinge."

"That's true, too," Sadie muttered.

Colin Farrell waited for them at the bottom of the stairs, whining and pacing, obviously upset that his new best friend was in trouble. Sadie scratched his ear and assured him he was a good boy and that everyone was fine.

"I swear, that dog knew what was going on. He cried about a minute before every contraction hit. He's a very smart, talented boy, aren't you, Colin Farrell? Yes, you are," Grace cooed at the dog, who preened and seemed to grow two inches taller under her praise.

This time Gage rolled his eyes as he set Grace on her feet by the front door. "He startles himself with his own farts. How smart and talented could he be?"

Grace smacked him in the chest with the back of her hand. "Don't be a dick. I'd think you'd be nicer, considering how you just got laid and all."

Gage remained stone-faced, but Sadie couldn't hold in a gasp. "How did you know?"

Grace gave her a satisfied smirk. "You just told me. Besides, when you guys left, you did *not* look like *that.*"

"Like what?" Gage demanded.

"Like you've been mauled by a bear." Grace gave them another quick once-over. "A horny bear."

Sadie glanced down at herself. Her dress looked like it'd been wadded up on the floor all night, and she could only imagine what her hair looked like.

And Gage hadn't escaped unscathed, either. His hair was sticking up in about twenty different directions, and was that a...*hickey* on his neck? Jesus, she didn't even remember giving him that, but since he also had her lipstick smudged all over his collar, it was pretty clear she was the culprit.

And, of course, the self-satisfied smirk on his face spoke *volumes* about what they'd been up to recently.

Sadie felt a full-body blush coming on. But there was no use denying it at this point. "Fine. Yes. We had hot, dirty sex in the back of Gage's car. Are you satisfied?"

Grace sighed. "No. Not really. I'm jealous more than anything. Pregnancy makes you horny as hell and my husband's been too scared to do much of anything to me for about a month now. I mean, sure, he'll give me all the oral I want, but no penetration. I think he's afraid he'll poke the baby in the eye while we're doing it or something."

"Oh, Jesus, kill me now," Gage muttered.

Grace just blinked up at him. "TMI?"

"Yes," Gage and Sadie said in stereo.

She shrugged. "Whatever. Wimps. And speaking of my hot husband, where is he?"

"An hour away," Sadie answered. "I'm not entirely sure he didn't commandeer a plane and a flight crew."

She was mostly kidding. But nothing Nick did would really surprise Sadie, either. He'd do anything for Grace, even if it meant breaking a few—or a few hundred—laws along the way.

Their devotion to each other was pretty awe-inspiring really.

Sadie still remembered what her brother had said five years ago when she asked him how anyone was supposed to know what love really was—how you knew if you'd found *the one*.

The one is the first person you think about when you wake up, and the last before you go to bed. You feel like a part of you is missing when you're not with her, like you can't quite catch your breath until she's there at your side. You hear a funny joke and the first thing you want to do is call her, because you know she'll think it's funny, too. She's the one who holds your heart in her hands, and the idea doesn't even scare you because you trust her with it and know there's no one else on earth you'd ever want to give it to, anyway. She makes you want to be better. At everything. She's…the balance.

It'd been that statement that helped her realize she couldn't marry Michael. She'd never felt that way—the way Nick felt about Grace—in her life.

Until now.

And that's when it hit her like a two-by-four to the gut. Her feelings for Gage didn't have anything to do with her old, instinctual need to cling to anyone who could offer her a family and a normal life. She wanted to cling to him just because he was…*him.*

She loved the way he grumped about what a pain in the ass Colin Farrell was, but then slipped him food off the table and told him he was a good boy when he thought she wasn't paying attention. She loved how he wasn't afraid to engage in a ridiculous debate about which TV characters would be the most handy to have around in case a zombie apocalypse broke out.

She loved how he'd cared for her when she was sick, even when her own fiancé wouldn't. She loved how he accepted her for exactly who she was, flaws and all.

She loved him.

This is what love was supposed to feel like. Gage Montgomery was *the one.*

"Holy shit," she muttered.

Two epiphanies in one night. That had to be a record or something.

Gage raised a brow at her. "You OK?"

The look of concern on his face was just further proof that he was freakin' perfect for her. God, she'd been such an idiot for insisting they stay friends for a respectable amount of time.

But after everything she'd put him through she couldn't just blurt it out on their way to the hospital, for God's sake. She'd have to pick the right moment. And preferably that moment wouldn't include a crazy pregnant lady.

So, she swallowed the love declaration that wanted to claw its way out of her throat and gave him a nod. "Yep. I'm fine. Oh, hey, look. The ambulance is here."

Gage gave her a look that let her know he didn't believe her for a second, but didn't push it. They quickly decided that Sadie would ride in the ambulance with Grace, and that Gage would follow.

"Should I call the rest of the family?" Sadie asked.

Grace and Gage groaned in stereo, then Gage said, "You won't have to. Ten-to-one they'll beat us to the hospital."

Sadie frowned. "How could they possibly?"

"Mom has spies everywhere," Grace answered, heart-attack serious. "She'll be there, and she will have called everyone before you can."

"You guys are exaggerating again," she said with a laugh.

Grace and Gage exchanged a look that Sadie couldn't quite interrupt before the ambulance doors shut.

CHAPTER TWENTY-FOUR

As it turned out, Grace's parents didn't beat the ambulance to the hospital. They got there twenty minutes later. They most likely *would* have beaten the ambulance, but they'd had to stop at the retirement home and pick up Grandma Ruthie on the way.

And now, they were all loitering in Grace's room, having just received the news that Grace was only three centimeters dilated and was nowhere near ready to start pushing.

It was going to be a long night.

Ruthie reached over and smacked her son, David, with her purse. "I told you there was no hurry! You pulled me out of wheelchair jazzercise for no reason."

Well, that explained her green tights, maroon leotard, and sparkly silver leg warmers, Gage thought.

Ruthie looked like a hundred year-old woman who'd been puked up by a Jane Fonda workout video from 1982.

David sighed and pushed his glasses up. "You're the one who told us to come get you, day or night, when it was time."

"Well, it's obviously not time," she groused. "And God knows when meal service will be. Who do you actually have to kill around here to get a Shasta and some green Jell-O?"

Grace's mom, Sarah, who looked more like Grace's older sister than her mother, shot Ruthie a harsh glare as she fluffed Grace's pillows for what must've been the thousandth time. "Keep complaining, old woman, and we'll ship you off to the retirement home we saw on *Dateline*."

Ruthie frowned at her. "I liked you better when you weren't so sassy. And even then I never really liked you."

From his chair at Grace's bedside, David, who'd apparently appointed himself as the adult in the room (which made sense because he was wearing a cardigan with leather elbow patches, and only a really adult-y adult could pull off *that* look), jabbed a stern finger at his mother: "Stop that." Then he turned the stern finger on his wife. "Both of you. You heard the doctor. Grace needs a stress-free environment for her delivery and that crap isn't helping."

Sarah looked contrite, but Ruthie just sniffed indignantly and said, "Kids today. Pfffttt. They're just weak, that's all. All this stress-free shit. Why, when I was pregnant, I never worried about being stress-free. You know what we did during childbirth? We sucked it up and didn't whine about it."

"And family wasn't allowed in the birthing room," Gage said. "I'm sure that helped."

"Amen," Grace mumbled. Then she glanced over at Sadie, who was perched on the arm of David's chair. "Have you heard from Nick?"

She nodded. "He's on his way. He'll be here any minute."

Gage didn't even want to think about how fast Nick must have driven from the airport to make that kind of time. Frankly, he half expected to get a call from Nick asking for bail money when he got caught breaking every speed limit in the state.

"Of course the Irishman's not here," Ruthie said. "I could've told you that would happen."

"You did tell her that," Sarah said. "Several times. But he's on his way. He'll be here soon."

"Sure he will," Ruthie said with a snort. "And I once had a torrid affair with Fidel Castro."

David raised his palms in the universal what-the-hell gesture and asked, "Why did your mind immediately go to *Fidel Castro* in that imaginary scenario? That's just weird, Mom."

"He wasn't bad looking back in the day," Ruthie said. "I would've hit that."

"Oh, God," Sarah said, sitting down on the corner of Grace's bed, dropping her forehead to her palm.

"Well, I would've," Ruthie added defensively. "He reminded me of the gardener my parents hired when I was eighteen. That boy really knew his way around my garden, if you know what I mean." She cackled.

"Oh, God," Gage said, horrified.

"And by garden," Ruthie said, "of course I mean my vagina."

Grace slammed her head back against her overly fluffed pillows and groaned. "Just shoot me now. Will someone please just shoot me now?"

Behind him, Gage heard Sadie try to cover a giggle with a

cough, but it came out more like a choked snort, which made him smile. Sarah must have seen it because she sat up straighter and pointed at him. "What is that?"

"What?"

She swirled her finger around, indicating his face. "The smile. The happy eyes. The lack of frown lines and sarcastic comments. What's this all about?"

Gage felt all eyes on him, but none were heavier than Sadie's. He had to fight every instinct in his body, all of which told him to look at her. This wasn't the time to out their relationship and make a big deal about it, he knew. Today was about Grace.

So, he merely shrugged and said, "Only in this family would happiness be a cause for suspicion."

Sarah's eyes narrowed on him. "I've never seen you happy. Not once in your life. Even when you were a little boy you were...dour. Like an Austen hero."

"Um...thanks?"

David eyed him up and down. "You do look...happy. It's a little weird, frankly."

He quickly wiped the smile off his face. "There. All better?"

Sarah shook her head. "Your eyes are still happy. What's going on with you?"

Ruthie snorted. "Are you people blind? He has a hickey the size of a cockroach on his neck. I'd say he's happy because he just got laid."

Don't look at Sadie. Don't look at Sadie. Don't. Look.At.Sadie...

Sarah gasped, then got a huge smile on her face and a speculative gleam in her eye that made him more than a little nervous. "Gage Montgomery, are you seeing someone?"

He shot a warning glance at Grace, who mimed zipping up her lips, then gave him a thumbs-up.

"Oh, come on," Sarah whined, "you have to give me *some* details. All I ever wanted was for you kids to be happy and find someone to settle down with so that you could start making grandbabies for me. And you never so much as even *hinted* at ever having a real relationship. I was starting to give up hope, honestly."

"We all thought you were gay and afraid to come out of the closet. You know, like that Tom Cruise fellow," Ruthie said.

"Not that there's anything wrong with that," Sarah was quick to add. "Gay men can always adopt babies and that'd be just fine with me."

Gage let his forehead drop to his palm. "Jesus, Sarah, I'm not gay."

"I could've told you that," David said, then scowled at Gage. "Don't think I never realized where all my *Playboys* went, you punk."

"I was a twelve-year-old boy. What did you expect? I couldn't exactly jack off to Sarah's JC Penney catalog."

"We all would've worried about you if you had," Grace muttered.

Sarah's brow furrowed. "What *Playboys*?"

David went pale, then smoothed out his features and said, "Hmm?"

YOU WRECKED ME / Isabel Jordan

She bristled. "Oh, don't you 'hmmm' me, mister. Did you keep porn in the house while the kids were still living there?"

"It's not porn," David and Gage said in unison, then frowned at each other.

"Oh, ease up, Sarah," Ruthie said. "Men need spank bank material. So do women, for that matter. Why, just the other day I was watching *Gladiator*, and let me tell you, young Russell Crowe has been a lovely addition to my spank bank. There's just something about that man in his battle armor that makes me—"

"Oh, Jesus," Grace muttered, her nose wrinkling up like she'd just taken a big whiff of sour milk. "I beg you not to finish that sentence."

"Second that," Gage piped up quickly.

Ruthie sniffed indignantly. "Prudes. There's nothing shameful about a woman's sexuality. Right, Sadie?"

All eyes turned to Sadie. She'd been laughing quietly at their conversation, but now that she was the center of attention, her laughter died down and she gulped hard. "Right," she answered carefully, slowly. "Of course there isn't."

Ruthie leaned forward in her wheelchair, her eyes narrowing on Sadie. More like on her neck, Gage realized.

Oh, shit.

Maybe Ruthie wouldn't say anything about it, he thought.

Yeah, no such luck.

"Is that a hickey on your neck, girl?"

Sadie's eyes widened and her hand flew to the spot on her neck that was indeed a hickey. If anyone had X-ray vision, they'd be able to see the other one he remembered leaving on he her. It was somewhere on the inside of her upper thigh.

Don't panic, he silently urged her. *And whatever you do, don't look at me.*

Her gaze flew to his, and Gage sighed. Well, so much for this being Grace's day.

But fate—or divine intervention—took charge in that moment, and before anyone could put two and two together (or, match up the two hickeys in the room), Grace let out a gasp that drew everyone's attention away from Sadie's neck.

"Are you OK?" Gage asked.

Grace's eyes were huge as she whispered, "My water just broke."

***

What followed was akin to a *Three Stooges* skit as everyone jumped up and scrambled to find a nurse. Gage ran to the nurse's station to have someone page Grace's doctor. Sadie called Nick to get his ETA. Sarah started pacing, obviously not sure what she could do while David went to get Grace a cup of ice chips.

About that time, a student nurse stuck her head in the room and said, "Your doctor is on his way. He'll be here in five. And, also…I'm thinking maybe the large, wild-eyed, armed man that hospital security just detained in the lobby belongs to you, too?"

"Big guy, blue eyes, probably totally frantic, looks a little like

Wolverine?

The girl nodded. "He's stupid hot."

Grace looked beyond relieved. "Yes, that's him. Can they do me a solid and not have him arrested? I kind of need him right about now."

Nick arrived a few minutes later at a dead run, skidding into the room like Kramer on *Seinfeld*. But while he looked to be about four hours past a five-o'clock shadow, had deep enough bags under his eyes to fit a week's worth of clothes in, and appeared to be running on nothing but caffeine and nerves, he took charge like a pro. He didn't hesitate to kick everyone out of Grace's room, for which she looked eternally grateful.

And now, five hours, four cups of crappy hospital coffee, and six games of gin rummy during which she learned that Grandma Ruthie cheated like a Vegas card shark, Sadie was standing at Grace's bedside, holding the brand-new baby.

Ellis Maria O'Connor came into the world at a whopping nine pounds, three ounces. She had a full head of midnight curls and the brightest blue eyes Sadie had ever seen. She also had a nice tight grip, Sadie noted, as Ellis wrapped her little fist around Sadie's pinkie and held on for dear life.

"I'm Auntie Sadie," she whispered to the tiny squirming burrito-wrapped bundle in her arms. "I'm going to buy you ice cream before dinner, and let you stay up all night when you visit, and give you pretty much anything you want that your parents won't give you."

"Great," an exhausted-looking Grace muttered from her

hospital bed. "Not even an hour old and you're already spoiling her rotten."

"It's my right—nay, my solemn duty—as an aunt to spoil this child."

Nick leaned forward and kissed his wife's forehead before giving Sadie a faux-stern look. "Remember, dear sister, that paybacks are a bitch. I'm not above invoking the same rights and loading your kids up with sugar and caffeine before sending them home with you."

Not too long ago, Sadie would've scoffed at the idea of having a squirming little bundle of her own. She was barely emotionally mature enough to take care of herself, let alone bring another little human into the world. But now? As she looked down into Ellis's beautiful blue eyes and felt that warm little hand gripping her own so tightly, it didn't seem so impossible.

"You've been quiet, Gage," Grace said. "What do you think? Isn't she gorgeous?"

"Absolutely," he murmured from his position in the doorway.

Sadie glanced up and found his warm gaze on her instead of the baby, and her ovaries immediately told her—no, *shouted* at her—that babies were indeed something she should consider.

"Not that I'm complaining," Nick said, "but it's awfully quiet in here. Where's everyone else?"

"Sarah and David went down to the gift shop to pick up something for Ellis," Gage said, "and the last time I saw Ruthie, she was stealing green Jell-O from the third-floor nurses' station."

"Pretty sure I just saw her trying to convince security that she's a patient," a new voice from behind Gage added.

Grace looked up and smiled a brighter-than-the-sun smile. "Michael! You made it!"

***

Gage turned and Michael gave him a handshake that ended in a back-slapping bro-hug. "Douchebag," Michael said in lieu of an actual greeting.

"Princess," Gage shot back.

A bro-hug for Nick followed, then Michael leaned down and gave Grace a real hug before turning to Sadie.

Gage watched Sadie's nerves start to get the better of her as she looked at the man she'd almost married. Her first love. The guy she'd left at the altar. She bit her lower lip and shifted her weight restlessly from one foot to the other.

"Michael," she said in the softest tone Gage had ever heard.

"Sadie."

Michael's tone was equally soft. They looked really good together, Gage realized with no small amount of distress. Michael's dark blonde curls and warm brown eyes were a perfect complement to Sadie's light-eyed, dark-haired beauty. He was everything Gage wasn't: open, social, friendly, and optimistic. Fun at parties and carrying absolutely zero emotional baggage. Michael was perfect for her. Way better for her than Gage could ever be.

What would he do if—when—Sadie realized that?

And suddenly Gage felt like that angry, lonely little eight-year-old that CPS dropped off on David and Sarah's doorstep all those years ago when his parents went out for drugs and never came home.

That day had just so happened to be the day after Michael's birthday. He had more toys than Gage had ever seen in real life and wore the smile of a kid who'd never had to steal bread from the grocery store because his parents had spent all their food money getting high. It had been damn hard not to resent a kid who'd been given everything he ever wanted.

And Gage could tell that Michael still wanted Sadie. It was written all over his face. Would this be yet another time when the universe handed Michael a prize and backhanded Gage for daring to want more?

Michael reached out and brushed his knuckles gently across Sadie's cheek and smiled at her. "You look good holding a baby," he said softly.

She let out a sharp breath and grinned back at him. "Everyone looks good holding *this* baby. She's crazy gorgeous."

"So true," Nick agreed.

Gage shifted his gaze to Grace, only to find her staring back at him with a look in her eyes that was dangerously close to pity, like she knew what he was thinking, how dark his thoughts had become.

Yeah, fuck *pity*.

He muttered something about running back to the house to check on the dog, turned on his heel, and fled the room like it was on fire, almost running into a nurse who was heading in, presumably to check on Grace and Ellis.

The nurse looked past him and smiled as she caught sight of Michael, who was now leaning close—way too close, in Gage's personal opinion—to Sadie as they both looked lovingly down at Ellis.

"Aw," the nurse cooed. "Aren't they just too cute together?"

Yep. Too cute. Just too fucking cute.

CHAPTER TWENTY-FIVE

"I thought I'd find you wherever the caffeine was."

Sadie jerked around so fast she almost spilled her brand new cup of crappy hospital coffee all over herself. "Jesus, Michael, you scared me. What are you doing out here?"

She'd figured out, oh, three or four cups of coffee ago that the nurses' station coffee was marginally less awful than the cafeteria coffee. And since she'd been sweet-talking the nurses and telling them how awesome they were all day, they were more than happy to let her steal a cup every now and then. But Michael didn't even drink coffee, so she wasn't sure why he'd be out here at all.

For some reason, that gave her a sick feeling in the pit of her stomach. It was a looming sense of dread, she realized. It was the same feeling she'd had right before her ill-fated wedding.

Michael shoved his hands in his pockets and shrugged. "I wanted to talk to you. Besides, Ellis is asleep and Grace and Nick were about to pass out, too. I thought they needed some peace and quiet."

She took a sip of her coffee and internally muttered every curse word she knew as the toxic brew scalded her tongue. "You wanted to talk to me? Is everything OK?"

He took a step toward her so that their chests were almost

touching, which made the sick feeling in her stomach intensify. She wanted to take a step back, but she was literally backed into a corner.

"Did you ever think that…" he shoved a hand through his hair like he always did when he was anxious, "…maybe we should've tried harder? That maybe if we'd, I don't know, gone to counseling or something that our relationship could've worked out?"

Sadie did more internal cussing. Son of a bitch, where was this coming from? They'd been broken up for five years. She'd left him at the altar, for God's sake! Why would he have even *wanted* to work things out with her after all that?

But instead of cussing at him, which he totally didn't deserve, she took a deep, cleansing breath and said, "Well…honestly, no. We were too young to be getting married, and after I left, I didn't think you'd want anything to do with me."

He looked down at his shoes. "Did you love me?"

She frowned. "You were my best friend! Of course I loved you."

"But you weren't…*in love* with me?"

Oh, boy. This one was tougher to explain.

She grabbed his hand and forced him to look her in the eye again. "Look, if I had been capable of being *in love* with anyone at that time, I would have been in love with you. You're smart and funny and hilarious and sexy, so of *course* I would have fallen for you. But the truth is that I didn't love *myself* back then. I didn't even really know who I was. I was always so busy trying to please everyone else that I never stopped to think about what *I* wanted. Who *I* wanted to be. I needed time. There's no way I could've loved anyone else when I didn't even love myself."

He rubbed his thumb over the back of her hand. "And now? Do you love yourself now?"

She smiled. "I do. It took me pretty much all this time to do it, but I think I've finally figured out who I am, and I like…me."

He gave her the crooked smile that had first drawn her to him all those years ago. "I could've told you how awesome you were. You should have asked me."

"That would have defeated the purpose, wouldn't it?"

"Maybe. But if you had, maybe we'd be together today. Maybe we would've been together all this time."

He got a look in his eye that made the *Star Trek* red alert siren go off in her head a split second before he murmured, "I've missed you so much" and moved in for a kiss.

Sadie yanked her hand out of his and slapped her palm against his chest, giving him a little shove back. "Whoa there, buddy. I'm sorry, but that's not happening."

He looked like a kicked puppy. "But…you said…I thought…shit, I got my hopes up and misread this whole thing, didn't I?"

She sighed and set her coffee down on the nurse's station counter. "Michael, I have no doubt that you're going to find someone who is perfect for you. Someone who, when you see her, makes you light up like Christmas morning. Someone who accepts you for exactly who you are and adores you, flaws and all. But…that person can't be

---

me. I'm so sorry."

He wanted to argue, she could tell, but he didn't. He looked resigned when he asked, "Is there someone else?"

Images of Gage flashed through her mind. His grumpy frown, his cocky smirk, the soft way he looked at her when he thought she couldn't see him, how he cared so fiercely about those he loved, but never wanted anyone to know just how much...yes, there was definitely someone else. She nodded and wasn't able to keep a stupid grin off her face.

Michael laughed. "Wow, OK. Now I get it. I never stood a chance because you're in love, right?"

The words made her sad, but thank God, he didn't sound bitter or angry. "I am," she answered quietly.

He was quiet for a moment, then nodded and said, "I'm sad for me, but I'm really happy for you, Sadie. You deserve all the happiness you can get in this world."

Tears sprung to her eyes at the sincerity in his tone. "Thank you so much. You're still a great friend, you know that?"

"You, too, Sades. I'm glad I knew you back then, and I hope you'll let me get to know who you've become." He held up his hands when she frowned a little. "In a totally platonic, friend-zoned way, of course."

She laughed and opened her arms to him. "Alright then, how about a totally platonic, friend-zoned hug, buddy?"

He snatched her up immediately in a bear hug that all but crushed her ribs. "Anytime, buddy."

And that's when Gage came around the corner and saw them.

CHAPTER TWENTY-SIX

Gage suddenly wished the hospital cafeteria sold vodka, because at the moment, he *really* felt like getting blind, stinking, falling-down drunk.

Because how else was he supposed to cope with seeing the woman he loved in Michael's arms? *Michael* who once had to be taken to the ER because he'd shoved an army man so far up his nose it had to be removed with surgical tools.

Gage still felt kind of bad about that, honestly. But how was he supposed to know the dumb little bastard would take a dare like that?

But that *so* wasn't the point right now.

The point was how good Michael and Sadie looked together. Smiling, happy, friendly, social people who looked like they were made for each other.

And seeing how happy Sadie looked as she hugged Michael? Well, that was a fucking double-edged sword. Because on the one hand, he wanted to be the one that put that smile on her face, not Michael, for God's sake. But on the other hand, Gage really *did* want Sadie to be happy. She deserved it. And if it was Michael who made her happy…so be it.

Gage would have to change his identity and start a new life in fucking Poland or Siberia or something, because there was no way in *hell* he'd ever be OK with seeing the two of them together again—all shiny and happy—on holidays and shit, but he could let her go if that's what she wanted. He wouldn't hold her back.

Even if it killed him.

That's when she looked up over Michael's shoulder and saw Gage standing there, frozen to the floor, staring pathetically at them, cup of forgotten coffee in his hand like a fucking loser.

This is where she'll give you a sympathetic head tilt, he thought. The oh-poor-delusional-Gage-thought-he'd-finally-get-to-be-happy head tilt. *Nope. No such luck, loser. You're gonna die alone, an old grumpy bastard who yells at the neighborhood kids to get off his lawn.*

But the look she *actually* gave him…well, it was *way* different than what he'd expected.

Her eyes met his and her already sunny smile grew until she was grinning at him. It was like she'd been waiting to see him all day. Like seeing him *made* her day. And to him, it felt like sunshine breaking through the clouds to shine down on him and only him. It was the best—and most confusing—feeling in the world.

She pulled back out of the hug, still aiming her sunny grin at Gage. God, she was pretty. He'd never get used to it.

In his peripheral vision—because he was still pretty much stuck in the tractor beam of Sadie's smile and couldn't look directly at anything else—he saw Michael follow Sadie's gaze.

And when that gaze landed on Gage, Michael muttered, "Light

up like Christmas morning."

That got Sadie's attention. Her smile drooped as she glanced back up at Michael. "Michael, I—"

"No," Michael interrupted, shaking his head. "Not *him*. Not this again. Tell me it's *anyone* but him."

She bit her lower lip and glanced back at Gage.

Gage still had no clue what was going on, but he didn't have time to ask, either. Because whatever answer Michael wanted to hear certainly wasn't the one Sadie was giving him. He looked back at Gage, furious.

"You son of a bitch," Michael said through clenched teeth.

And with that, he vaulted over the nurses' station counter and grabbed Gage in a flying tackle, dragging him to the ground. Coffee and papers and office supplies scattered all around them as Michael started throwing wild punches.

"Jesus Christ," Gage gasped as he blocked as many of Michael's haymakers as he could. "What the fuck is the matter with you?"

Even though Michael was an inch or two shorter than Gage and at least twenty pounds lighter, the kid had enough rage on his side to get the upper hand and catch Gage off guard with solid hit across his cheekbone. Gage felt his skin split, which really pissed him off.

"I don't want to hurt you, Michael," Gage said as he blocked more punches and tried to throw Michael off him, "but calm the fuck down or this is going to get ugly."

"You just couldn't stay away from her, could you?" Michael

ground out. "I'll kill you!"

There pretty much wasn't any reasoning with him after that. For the next God-knows-how-many minutes, they rolled on the hospital floor, fists flying. They kept hitting each other as the crowd around them got bigger and people tried to pull them apart. Gage heard Sadie's voice above the others, pleading with them to stop.

And Gage wanted to stop. Really, he did. He didn't want to hurt Michael and he didn't want to upset Sadie, but Michael kept swinging, so he did the same. Over and over again.

Until the cops showed up, yanked them apart, and hauled them off to jail.

***

"Well, that was a shit show of epic proportions," Ruthie said.

If someone had asked Gage to name the top five people who were most likely to show up after he'd been arrested and visit him in his jail cell, Ruthie wouldn't have made the list. Not even in the top five, actually. But here she was, sitting outside the cell, shaking her head at him.

Gage just lifted his head from his hands and glanced at her, but Michael jumped up and raced to the bars, reaching for her like she was his lifeline. "Are you here to get us out? Please tell me you're here to get us out. I can't take it in here anymore."

Gage rolled his eyes. They were sitting in a county drunk tank, for God's sake, not Shawshank. By his estimation, they'd been there for about two hours, but to hear the desperation in Michael's voice, you'd think they were five years into a ten- year stretch.

"I came to sweet-talk the cops into letting you go," Ruthie said.

Gage snorted at the idea of Ruthie sweet-talking anyone, but Michael threw himself back down onto one of the concrete slab benches at the back of the cell and whined, "Oh, God, we're gonna die in here!"

Ruthie rolled her eyes. "Relax, Princess. Sadie came with me. She's filling out some paperwork and you'll be out of here in a few minutes. No one wants to keep you idgits here. You're lucky, too. You'd never survive in prison, Michael. You'd be someone's bitch within an hour." Then she glanced at Gage. "And you'd be an asshole to someone and get shanked in the shower."

She wasn't wrong, he realized. But that wasn't his concern at the moment.

"Is she OK?" he asked Ruthie quietly.

Ruthie frowned at him. "Sadie? She's mad enough to eat nails and spit tacks. It's kinda cute, really. Like Bambi, but if Bambi got rabies."

Gage failed to see what was cute about Bambi with rabies, but he'd learned long ago not to question Ruthie too much. Most of the time, her clarifications were more confusing than anything she said the first time around.

"But I'm not here about Bambi," Ruthie said. "I'm here so that you two fuckwits can get your crap together before she comes back here. You're not getting out of this cell until you can act like adults."

Gage crossed his arms over his chest. "All I did was walk down the damn hall. That ass clown is the one who tackled me."

Michael leaned forward on his bench and glared at Gage. "You stole my fiancée, asshole. You're lucky all you ended up with was a few bruises."

He gingerly felt the cut on his cheek. "And a cut that's probably going to scar. Thanks a lot for that."

"Did you miss the part about stealing my fiancée? You deserve that scar."

Ruthie waved a hand dismissively. "Scars are hot. Everyone knows that. You'll be lucky to have it. Frankly, you're too pretty without it. The boy did you a favor."

Michael harrumphed, looking so superior that Gage itched to smack him around again. But Ruthie shut Michael down with, "And I wouldn't look so smug, boy. You got lucky with that punch because you were windmilling like a damn fool. Worst fight I've ever seen. I didn't take you two to all those hockey games to watch you sissy-fight like a couple of drunk southern belles who accidentally wore the same dress to a cotillion."

Gage wasn't even going to try and figure out what *that* meant, so he addressed Michael instead. "I didn't steal your fiancée. Mostly because she hasn't been your fiancée for five years."

Michael shot him a mulish look and mimicked Gage's posture, crossing his arms over his chest. "She ran away five years ago because of you."

"Oh, that's bullshit and you know it. She ran away because you were way too young to get married and she didn't really understand

YOU WRECKED ME / Isabel Jordan

what she wanted from life. It had nothing to do with me."

His eyes narrowed. "There was something going on between the two of you back then. I felt it. You can't tell me it wasn't there."

Gage threw his hands up in exasperation. "I wanted her, OK? That shouldn't shock you. She's the most perfect woman I've ever laid eyes on. Of course I wanted her. But I never would've done anything about it back then. And I didn't go after her. We ran into each other by accident five years later, for fuck's sake. I wouldn't have hurt you like that. I'm a dick, but I'm not *that* much of a dick."

Michael looked like he wanted to argue the point further, but eventually blew out a defeated sigh. "I know that. Deep down, I know that. And she wouldn't have hurt me like that, either. But when I saw the way she looked at you today...I just lost it, OK? I hadn't seen her in so long, and she looked so perfect, standing there, holding Ellis, that I guess I let nostalgia get the better of me." He shoved his hand through his hair. "It's stupid, but I thought maybe I could get another chance with her. It was hard enough hearing that she was in love with some other guy, but to find out that other guy was *you*? The guy who made me shove an army man up my nose when I was six? It was just more than I could handle."

Gage sat up straighter. *She said she was in love with me?*

He'd have to let that info marinate for a minute. It was too early to get his hopes up at this point. After the childish display she'd witnessed at the hospital, he wouldn't blame her if she decided she was done with him and his insane family forever.

"In my defense," Gage said, "you were a really gullible six-year-old. Grace never would've done it."

"Everyone knows that only pussies ignore the double dog dare," Ruthie interjected. "Michael had no choice but to try. I commend him for taking it to the next level and lodging GI Joe that far up into his sinuses."

Gage gave her a pointed look. "I double dog dare you to shut up and let us hash this out ourselves."

She pursed her lips and shot him a you've-won-this-round-but-I'll-get-you-next-time glare. Then she gave him the finger.

"Sorry I messed up your perfect face," Michael said with a barely there half-smile.

"Sorry about the kidney punch."

He nodded. "I'm going to be pissing blood for a week, I think."

"Probably only three days. I didn't hit you *that* hard."

"Dick," Michael said, his half-smile morphing into something more genuine.

"Bitch," Gage shot back, biting down on a smile of his own.

Ruthie sniffled and pulled a tissue out of her bra and dabbed at her eyes. "That was so beautiful."

"Are we good?" Gage asked.

"Yeah, we're good, man." Michael's gaze turned serious again. "Do you love her?"

Gage didn't even hesitate. "I do. More than anything."

Michael glanced down at his bruised knuckles and nodded. "That's good. She deserves to be happy and loved. So do you."

He couldn't agree more. Gage just hoped she'd give him the

chance to love her and make her happy.

CHAPTER TWENTY-SEVEN

Sadie wasn't sure what she'd find when the officer walked her back to the cell, but of all the possible scenarios, seeing Michael and Gage sitting next to each other on a concrete bench, behind bars, talking and laughing while they each still bore the bruises they'd given each other…well, that picture hadn't entered her mind.

Men. So freakin' weird.

Ruthie glanced up at her as she approached and said, "I fixed them, honey. You're welcome. Now you can pick your guy and go home and forget this bullshit ever happened. I'd pick carefully if I was you. Gage is a grumpy bastard, but he has good earning potential. And Michael is loyal like a little puppy dog, even though he punches like a pansy. So, I'd think it over and wouldn't make any knee-jerk decisions if I was you."

"Um…thanks?"

Ruthie reached over and patted her hand. "My pleasure, dear. Now, I'm going to find a doughnut."

And with that, she wheeled off, leaving Sadie alone with her idiot ex-fiancé and the sexy idiot she was in love with.

So, *so* much awkward.

There was no point in beating around the bush, she supposed.

It's not like avoiding the obvious would make things less awkward. So, she took a deep breath and let the verbal diarrhea fly. "Look, I'm just going to say this, so I need both of you to shut up and just listen. Don't say a word until I'm done. I mean it, not a word, not a smartass look," she paused to glare at Michael, "not a smartass smirk," she paused to glare at Gage, "nothing."

Gage and Michael exchanged a look before returning their attention to her, but it wasn't a smartass-y look, so she let it go. "Michael, I'm going to start with you because what I feel for you is way less complicated than what I feel for him," she said, jerking her thumb in Gage's direction. "You already know you were probably the best friend I've ever had and I did—still do—love you, but we broke up and haven't seen each other in five years. You have no right to be jealous seeing me with someone else. None at all. We've been done for a long time. I wasn't the one for you, and deep down you know it. And I want us to be friends again, but if you pick fights with the man I love every time you see me with him, I'm going to kick your ass. I mean it, Michael. I'm going shove my foot so far up your ass you'll be tasting the soles of my Chucks for the rest of your life."

Michael didn't say anything, but Gage stood up and moved across the cell. He rested his elbows on the horizontal bar that crossed the cell door and leaned there casually, but there wasn't anything casual about the look on his face. That's when it occurred to her that she'd just called him the man she loved without first telling *him* he was the man she loved.

She threw her hands up. "Goddamn it! I wasn't supposed to

say that until I was ready to yell at you! I wasn't ready yet!"

"You love me," he murmured.

Sadie moved to the bars and poked him in the chest with her index finger. "I saw the look on your face when you saw me hugging Michael. After everything, you *really* thought I might leave you and go back to him, didn't you?"

The smartass brow lifted. "You love me."

Another poke. "You really doubted me, didn't you?"

He grabbed her finger and tugged her closer. "You. Love. Me."

She scowled at him. "Of course I love you, you dumbass! I've been searching for myself for the past five years, and it turns out that I'm more *me* when I'm with you than I am with anyone else."

He gave her a look, silently asking her if he could speak. She rolled her eyes and said, "Yes, now it's your turn."

"I spent my whole life putting up walls to keep people out because I was sure, so sure, that everyone would eventually let me down." He laced their fingers together and the contact—and the intense look in his eyes—made her tremble. "I never expected anyone to prove me wrong or make me regret those walls. But that's exactly what you did, Sadie. You completely wrecked me. And I love you for it. I just…" he took a deep breath. "I love you. I've never said that to anyone before in my life, not even family, but I love you, Sadie."

And just like that, her anger evaporated and she'd never felt so happy in her life. "I really want to kiss you right now but I also kind of don't want to touch these gross bars," she whispered.

"You shouldn't," Ruthie said from behind them as she two-

YOU WRECKED ME / Isabel Jordan

fisted doughnuts. "Officer Anus here said they had a masturbator in there yesterday. Probably got jizz everywhere."

And *splat* went their romantic moment. *Thanks, Ruthie.*

The officer sighed as he unlocked the cell door. "It's pronounced, *Ahn-us,*" he said in a long-suffering tone.

Ruthie shook her head. "No, that's how *you* pronounce it. To everyone else, you're Officer Anus. Own it. Be proud of your awful last name. It'll make you a stronger person."

"Wow, you are just full of sage advice today, old woman," Michael muttered.

But Sadie ignored them all as Gage stepped out of the cell, into her arms, and proceeded to kiss the crap out of her. He seemed to be pouring every emotion he'd been bottling up all his life into the kiss, and she kissed him back with everything she had.

She loved him.

He loved her.

They finally—finally—got their timing right. It was a damn miracle!

He was the first to break the kiss, and when he pulled back to rest his forehead against hers, they were both breathing hard. "I'm going to marry you," he whispered.

She grinned, even though she knew she was on the hairy edge of an ugly cry. "Is that a question?"

"It's a promise."

Sadie put her hand on his heart and let out a watery chuckle. "I'm going to hold you to that."

And she fully intended to do just that. Because the life she'd been wanting for all these years? It was finally about to start. After all these years of wandering aimlessly, she'd finally found the one thing she'd been longing for all her life: a home where she truly belonged. And that home was wherever Gage Montgomery was.

He gave her the grin she loved best—the crooked one that he reserved for her and her alone. "So, where do we go now? Back to Grace's place? Montana? Somewhere else? I'd follow you anywhere."

"It totally doesn't matter," she said, then grabbed him and kissed him again. "This is the best day I've ever had."

He pulled her tighter against him and looked down at her with those intense eyes she loved so much and said, "No way, sweetheart. The best days are yet to come."

The End

But if you missed Grace and Nick's story, keep flipping through some pages, because the whole first chapter is included! (There also might be a full chapter of book 1 of the Harper Hall Investigations series in there somewhere…if you're into that kind of thing…) Happy reading!

A personal note from Isabel:

If you enjoyed this book, first of all, thanks! It would mean a lot to me if you would take a moment and show your support of indie authors (like me) by leaving a review. Your reviews are a very important part of helping readers discover new books.

Want to know more about me, or when the next book release is? You can email me directly at: isabel.jordan@izzyjo.com.

Thanks so much, and happy reading!

Sample of *You Complicate Me*

CHAPTER ONE

In retrospect, the Valium probably would've been enough to soothe Grace Montgomery's nerves on the flight from Los Angeles to Indianapolis. The wine was most likely overkill.

As was the tequila.

It had all started innocently enough. "Take one pill an hour before the flight," her doctor had told her, "and one an hour into the flight. You'll be completely relaxed. Valium is magic, I swear."

"The kind of magic that keeps planes from falling from the sky in a ball of fiery death?" Grace had asked.

Her doctor's answering smirk should've been a warning. "The kind of magic that makes you not care on the way down."

And she hadn't. Cared, that is. The magic Valium had done its job.

Until take-off, at least.

As soon as the plane started rolling down the runway, as soon as she felt the rumbling of the engine in her belly, she started panicking. The man sitting next to her in seat C2, no doubt having noticed the white-knuckled grip she had on their adjoining armrest, had suggested a glass of wine, which she'd requested from the flight attendant as soon as she'd been allowed. But even though she gulped it down in two swallows, the wine was absolutely no match for her anxiety, because she soon started hyperventilating.

C2 had pressed an air-sickness bag into one of her hands, and a mini bottle of tequila into the other. After breathing deeply into the bag for a few moments, she'd unscrewed the tequila and downed it, too. One swallow that time.

Grace was nothing if not a quick learner.

It was then she'd made what she thought was a tragic error. She'd asked for a second bottle of tequila, which she used to wash down her second Valium. The calm that had quickly washed over her was amazing. She couldn't remember a time when she'd felt so relaxed.

And warm. She was suddenly really, really, warm. So it only made sense that she'd strip off her sweater, right?

Sadly, while she was shedding layers, she elbowed the guy next to her in the eye.

"Jesus Christ," he'd muttered, holding a hand over one eye.

That was when she got her first good look at C2.

Maybe it was the Valium, or maybe it was the alcohol, but holy hell, he was *beautiful.*

His inky hair was long overdue for a trim and fell in messy disarray—the kind of messy disarray that hot men achieved naturally and women paid big bucks to a salon to fake—to just above the collar of his white button-down shirt. With his knife-edged cheekbones, strong jaw, and olive complexion, he looked like he could be Hugh Jackman's younger brother.

Grace had watched *Wolverine* four times, and not because the storyline was stellar (or even remotely plausible, really). Her mouth immediately went dry. Other parts of her…not so much.

"I'm r-really sorry," she whispered.

He lowered his hand and she winced at the elbow-sized welt forming under his eye. "Are you always like this on a plane?" he asked.

"Like what?"

"Fucking crazy?"

She frowned at him. "I'm a nervous flyer, okay? Lots of people are nervous flyers."

He shook his head and ran his hand through that amazing hair of his. "This isn't nervous. I've seen nervous. You're a train wreck, lady."

He wasn't lying. Didn't make his comment any less insulting. "I'm sorry if my fear of falling from the sky and plummeting to a fiery death is inconveniencing you in any way."

One black brow winged upward. "Fear all you want. I couldn't care less. But when you try to blind me with your fucking elbow while you strip down to your underwear…well, that's when I start to care."

Grace glanced down at her white layering tank top. It wasn't see-through. Minimal cleavage was on display. Perfectly respectable. "I said I was sorry about elbowing you, okay? And I'm not in my underwear."

His gaze dipped down. "I can tell that you're cold." He smirked as his eyes met hers again. "Or turned on."

She *so* wasn't cold.

"I'm cold," she said dryly. "Don't flatter yourself."

His smirk morphed into a full-fledged grin, and Grace fought

YOU WRECKED ME / Isabel Jordan

the urge to fan herself. Jesus, the grin was nothing short of panty-dropping. A smile like that should be illegal. All those straight white teeth and the dimple that carved into his cheek…it was gratuitous, really.

And his eyes? An amazing oceanic mix of blue and pale green. Men shouldn't be allowed to have eyes that pretty.

"Let's start over," he said. He held out his hand. "I'm Nick. Nick O'Connor."

She was so busy staring at his eyes—and being envious of his thick, dark eyelashes, if she was being honest with herself— that it took her a moment to realize he was speaking to her. She took his hand. "Grace. Grace Montgomery."

Something akin to recognition lit his eyes for a moment, making her wonder if he knew her. Had they met before? But she immediately dismissed the thought. If she'd met *this* guy before, she'd remember it.

His hand was warm and callused, and dwarfed hers. Her gaze traveled from his hand up his thick forearm, exposed by the rolled-up sleeve of his shirt. His biceps strained the fabric of that shirt, as well. If the arms were any indication, a muscly chest and flat stomach were a foregone conclusion.

She considered then that her judgment might be impaired. No one was *this* good-looking. Or else Nick O'Connor was genetically blessed in a way that was totally unfair to all other men.

Tequila goggles. She was wearing a set of tequila goggles. There was no other explanation.

He cleared his throat, drawing her attention back to his face. He let go of her hand and she fought the urge to grab his again. She knew she was an embarrassment to feminists everywhere, but there was something insanely comforting about having a big, strong guy holding her hand. If she'd grabbed him early on, maybe she wouldn't have needed the Valium. Or wine. Or tequila.

"So, Grace," he said, "have you always been a nervous flyer?"

She laid her head back against the seat, suddenly feeling a little off balance. "Yeah. I don't like being closed in. Or depending on people I don't know to fly the plane. And land the plane."

"Uh huh. So you're one of *those*."

She frowned at him again. "One of those *what?*"

"Control freaks."

"I am not a control freak."

Was it her imagination, or had she slurred that sentence?

He gave her the panty-dropping grin again. Yep, she'd slurred.

"Whatever you say, angel."

Being called a control freak was kind of a hot button for Grace. It was something her ex-husband never failed to bring up when they'd argued, which had been often. And the fact that this total stranger would agree with her ex pissed her off. She also took exception to him assigning her a nickname. Grace unbuckled her seatbelt and stood up to tell him so.

And that's when her memory got a little...fuzzy.

She had a distinct memory of poking him in the chest, telling him he didn't know anything about her. He'd told her to sit down. To *calm* down. She'd refused, colorfully and loudly. She'd tried to badger a man in another row into trading seats with her. The guy had refused, colorfully and loudly.

Nick had gotten in the middle of that argument and tried to tell her something about who he was, what his job was, but she was too busy yelling about…something to catch all of it.

The next thing she knew, Nick had forced her back into her seat. He might've also threatened to cuff her if she got into any other arguments with passengers, which seemed a little excessive. And…kinky.

"I'm sorry," she thought he'd said at that point.

"I'm sorry, too," she vaguely remembered responding.

Then, she couldn't be sure, but she thought she might have leaned over and puked all over his shoes. After that…there was nothing but blissful, blissful unconsciousness.

Like it so far? You can download today from Amazon. Happy reading!

Sample of *Semi-Charmed*, book 1 in the Harper Hall
Investigations Series

CHAPTER ONE

Whispering Hope, New York, today

Harper Hall swatted the fast-fingered hand of yet another
horny, middle-aged CPA off her ass, but resisted the urge to dump
tequila in this one's lap. After all, the Prince Valiant haircut and
underbite he was saddled with were punishments enough for his
crimes.

"Hey, baby," Valiant's friend said as he fondled his shot glass
suggestively. "Is that a mirror in your pocket? 'Cause I can definitely
see myself in your pants."

Harper rolled her eyes and shot back, "Darlin', I'm not your
type. I'm not inflatable."

And with that, she turned on the heel of one of her requisite
six-inch platforms and started for the bar as the CPAs chortled and
bumped knuckles. They were probably looking at her butt too, but
Harper chose not to dwell on that, or on the fact that most of said butt
was probably hanging out of her Daisy Dukes. Not her best look, to
be sure.

Lanie Cale, one of the other waitresses, grabbed her arm and
leaned in, shouting over the music, "Hey, can you take over for me

YOU WRECKED ME / Isabel Jordan

with the guy at table five? Carlos is letting me dance tonight. I go on in ten."

Harper gave her a quick once over. Lanie was five years her junior, ten pounds lighter, and had her beat by a full cup size. If she was Lanie, she'd probably aspire to be a stripper too. But as it stood, she was stuck waiting tables with the other B-cups.

"Sure," she answered. "But, Lanie, this guy at table five...he's not a CPA, is he? I don't think I have the strength for another CPA."

"No *way* is this guy a CPA. I'd bet Hugh Jackman's abs on it," she promised solemnly as she disappeared into the crowd.

At that moment, the sweaty throng of dancers and customers and waitresses parted, giving Harper her first glimpse of the guy at table five.

Wow. Hugh Jackman's abs were in no danger tonight.

The guy at table five was definitely *not* an accountant. Serial killer, maybe. CPA...um, no.

Table five was wedged in the corner, to the *extreme* right of the stage, which was why no one usually wanted to sit there. But instinct told Harper this guy had refused to sit anywhere else. This was one of those never-let-anyone-sneak-up-behind-you types, maybe with a military or law enforcement background. Paranoid and probably with good reason.

Everything about him screamed tall, dark, and brooding. From the black hair long overdue for a trim to the black-on-black wardrobe, complete with biker boots and a *Highlander*-like leather trench, this guy was either a true rebel without a cause, or the best imitation of one she'd ever seen.

And he was drunk off his ass. Not the kind of happy, silly drunk the CPAs at table ten had going. No, Harper could tell by the way he was ignoring the half-naked dancer on stage that he was drowning his sorrows.

Ignoring Misty Mountains wasn't easy, either. Her brand new double D's were mesmerizing, and the nipples kind of followed you wherever you went like the eyes on the creepy Jesus picture in her mom's living room.

As Harper watched, he polished off a bottle of Glenlivet and set it beside two other empties. She sighed. He'd probably pass out before he remembered to tip her. God damn drunks would be the death of her.

Harper squared her shoulders and walked up to the table, then knelt beside him so he could hear her over the bassline of Bon Jovi's *Lay Your Hands On Me.*

"Can I get you anything else, sir? Like coffee?" *Hint, hint.*

He didn't even glance at her as he slid the empty bottles to the edge of the table and said, "Another bottle."

His voice sent a shiver down her spine. It was gravelly, raspy, almost like he'd growled the words instead of speaking them. *Sexy.*

But sexy voice or not, she wasn't about to serve him another bottle. He was probably a few inches over six feet and maybe a little over two-hundred pounds, but no one—not even a manly man like this one—could down four bottles of eighteen-year-old Glenlivet and blow a Breathalyzer that wouldn't get him immediately arrested.

"I think you've probably had enough for tonight."

He slowly glanced over at her as if he hadn't really noticed her presence until just then. When her eyes locked with his, she completely forgot what they'd been talking about. Hell, who was she kidding? She forgot how to *breathe*.

This had to be the most gorgeous potential serial killer she'd ever seen.

He had a dark olive complexion most women would kill for, cheekbones sharp enough to cut glass, and eyes that were either black or the deepest blue she'd ever seen—it was too dark in the club to tell for sure.

His perfectly arched black brows—and they had to be naturally perfect, because she was pretty sure this guy wouldn't be caught dead waxing—raised sardonically as his gaze moved over her.

Harper fought the urge to suck in her stomach and desperately wished her uniform was a size eight instead of a four. She had dignity in a size eight. Class, even. In a four...not so much.

He lowered his gaze to her chest, and then slowly lifted it back to her eyes. "I doubt they're paying you to think, sunshine." Sliding the empty bottles even closer to her, he repeated, "Another bottle."

He'd said it very slowly, deliberately, in a manner most people reserved for slow-witted children and foreigners. The only part of her that wasn't at all impressed with the guy's fallen-angel face—which just happened to be her Sicilian temper—kicked in at that point.

Harper straightened and snagged the bottles off the table, preparing to verbally flay him, but just when she'd figured out exactly how many four-letter words she could hurl at him in one sentence, a premonition hit her hard.

People often asked her what premonitions felt like. Imagine someone punching a hole through your forehead and making a fist around your brain, she always told them. This premonition was no different.

Harper staggered forward and planted one palm on the table to steady herself as images assailed her: a young, blonde woman in an alley pinned to a dumpster by a man twice her size.

A vampire, she knew instinctively. Cold chills always shot down her spine when she saw them.

Harper sucked in a deep breath and forced herself to concentrate on details other than the victim, just like Sentry taught her so many years ago. Instead, she tried to picture the dumpster, the buildings around it, street signs…anything that might tell her where this girl was so she could call the police and get her some help.

And then she saw a logo printed on the side of the dumpster as big as life. *Kitty Kat Palace.*

Holy shit, the vamp and his victim were *here.*

Harper staggered back toward the kitchen, shoving drunks and other waitresses out of her way. In the kitchen, she tipped a wooden stool on its side and stomped on one of the legs.

She bent down and scooped it up, testing its weight in her hand. Not the best stake, but it would do. Hopefully.

Normally in a situation like this, Harper would let Romeo go after the vamp first, then help him if necessary. After all, slayers, even crappy ones like Romeo, were ten times stronger than the average human, and unfortunately, being a seer didn't afford her any supernatural strength.

But Romeo—the rat bastard—was probably at the Bellagio, hip-deep in hookers and craps winnings at the moment.

Harper heard the woman scream as she kicked the back door open and stumbled into the alley.

Just like in her premonition, a biker-clad vampire had the small woman pinned up against the dumpster with the weight of his body, one beefy arm across her shoulders, his other hand clutching her jaw so that he had a clear shot at her jugular.

Harper's heart clawed its way up to her throat as she met the woman's horror-filled gaze. She could practically taste the woman's fear.

She swallowed hard and forced herself to break eye contact, taking stock of the situation. Her gaze flicked over the vampire.

The vamp had at least eight inches and a hundred pounds on her. This could be a problem, common sense told her.

But as usual, her mouth didn't listen to common sense. "Hey, asshole."

The vampire raised his head from the woman's throat, a crimson ribbon of blood dribbling down his chin. Cute.

"Why don't you pick on someone more my size."

Okay, so it was a line she'd picked up from watching *Buffy the Vampire Slayer* reruns. Witty repartee should never be wasted, even if it wasn't original.

He laughed, a hollow, cold sound that slithered up and down her spine, leaving goose bumps in its wake. "Run while you still can, little girl."

She shook her head and clucked her tongue. "I don't think so, Vlad. Running? Not so much a good idea in these shoes."

His fangs slowly retracted like a cat's claws, making him look almost human. Almost.

"I like a girl with spirit," he said. "Enhances her flavor."

"Wow, that was almost clever. I'm shocked. I had you pegged as stupid *and* ugly. Maybe I can upgrade you to just ugly."

Harper had forgotten how fast a motivated vampire could move. One second he was ten feet away, and half a heartbeat later, he stood close enough to backhand her.

And backhand her he did. For him it was careless, effortless. Like swatting a fly. It was still enough to fill her mouth with blood and knock her on her ass.

From her position on the ground, she noticed the blond still frozen in place against the dumpster. "Run," she mouthed.

Obviously in shock, the blond stared at her as if she hadn't noticed, and this time Harper shouted, "Run!"

The girl finally seemed to snap out of her stupor. She spun on her heel and fled down the alley.

Harper breathed a sigh of relief as she shakily climbed to her feet and faced a very large, very angry vampire.

Yipes.

"Bitch," he said through clenched teeth, "I'm gonna take you apart piece by piece."

Again, common sense wasn't Harper's co-pilot as she spat back, "Gee, that might be scary if I didn't already know you hit like a girl."

This time when he swung at her, she was ready for him. Harper kicked out as he lunged for her, catching him in the knee with her gold platforms.

He went down with a yelp. "You bitch!"

"Now, I'm getting real sick of you calling me that."

Harper tried to kick him in the face, but he was too fast for her. He grabbed her ankle and yanked it out from under her. She landed on her butt with an unladylike grunt.

God, where was a good crossbow when she really needed one?

He was on her before she could scramble to her feet, pinning her to the ground with his weight. She managed to free one of her hands and gouged his eye, gagging a little as her thumb sunk in up to the knuckle.

The vampire screeched and leapt off her, one hand pressed to what was left of his eye.

Harper stood up and raised the stake. "Now, I don't want to kill you, but I will if I have to. If you run away now, we can forget this whole thing ever happened."

He whipped a wicked-looking hunting knife out of his jacket pocket. "You're gonna die slow."

Harper took a big step back. So much for diplomacy.

But before she could come up with any other bright ideas, someone moved up fast behind her and shoved her out of the way. She hit the ground again.

Being a hero certainly wasn't all it was cracked up to be. Very hard on the tush.

"Who the fuck are you?" the vamp yelled, clutching the knife in one hand and his eye with the other.

"Death," the newcomer answered dryly.

Harper's head shot up. She'd know that voice anywhere.

Standing a few feet away from her, presenting her with his impressive profile, was Mr. Congeniality himself: the gorgeous, potential serial-killer from table five.

On a happier note, Harper realized that Mr. Personality was at least a head taller than the vamp and seemed to have more muscle weight. That might even the odds a little for the home team, she decided.

The vamp took a step back and raised his hands, suddenly all friendly and peace-loving. "Look, man, I got no problem with you."

Harper snorted. "Who's the bitch now, you big pussy?"

She slapped a hand over her mouth. Damn it, she hadn't meant to say that out loud.

Her savior glanced over at her and that was all the time the vamp needed. He swung out wildly, slicing neatly into Table Five's stomach. Harper gasped as blood quickly dampened the fabric of his T-shirt.

But the wound didn't even seem to faze Table Five. He caught the vamp's fist when he took his next shot and used his momentum to pull him closer, then drove his knee into the vampire's stomach. The vampire dropped to his knees, arms wrapped around his middle as he coughed and gagged. Table Five kicked out without hesitation, catching the vamp in the chin, knocking him flat on his back.

Table Five yanked him up by the hair and twisted his arm behind his back. A sound akin to a dry twig snapping was closely followed by another pained groan from the vampire.

Harper blinked. It took a hell of a lot of strength to break a vampire's bones. An *unnatural* amount of strength. This guy did it without even trying. Who the hell was he?

"Quit whining," Table Five growled at the now blubbering vampire, then gave him a good swift kick in the ass. "And get the hell out of here while I'm still in a good mood."

Harper kept her eyes on the vamp until he'd stumbled out of view, then turned her attention to the man who'd saved her life. The man who'd just reduced a violent vampire to tears.

"Who are you?" she asked suspiciously. "And don't say *Death*."

He glanced at her and the street light allowed her to see his eyes were blue. Deep, deep blue. Gorgeous, she thought, then mentally slapped herself for noticing something so trivial after what had just happened.

He paused as if contemplating not telling her his name, but eventually said, "Call me Riddick."

Harper realized she was still on the ground and slowly climbed to her feet. All her parts seemed to be in working order, and she hadn't peed herself. She supposed she couldn't really ask for more than that, given the circumstances.

"Riddick?" she repeated. "Like the Vin Diesel movies?"

He stared at her like she was deranged. Must not be a Vin Diesel fan.

Then it occurred to her where she'd heard the name before, and Vin Diesel had nothing to do with it. "Are you *Noah* Riddick? The slayer?"

He wadded up the fabric at the hem of his T-shirt and pressed it to his wound. "There aren't any more slayers."

She rolled her eyes. Slayers and seers hadn't fallen off the face of the earth when Sentry disbanded and vamps earned human rights. They might be jobless, but they still existed. "I'm thinking the vamp with the broken arm still believes in slayers."

Noah Riddick in Whispering Hope, Harper thought when he didn't respond. What were the odds?

Whispering Hope had been settled largely by Italian, Polish and Irish immigrants who hadn't enjoyed big city life, which accounted for the fact that there were a ton of great restaurants in her beloved town, but no industry to speak of. And it was too far away from the *real* city for convenience, so truly, the only reason Harper could think of for anyone who wasn't born in Whispering Hope to settle here was the food.

But she'd just bet that Noah Riddick wasn't in town for a kolache from Majesky's on High Street.

Riddick adjusted his makeshift compress and she stared at his bare stomach, not sure if she was more fascinated by the wound—which was pumping out a surprising amount of blood—or by his perfect abs.

She cleared her throat. "We should probably get you to a hospital. That stomach looks hot…er, I mean it looks like it *hurts*."

Sweet Christ, could she humiliate herself in front of this guy a few *more* times?

"I don't do hospitals," he said.

Great. A macho man. Just what she needed more of in her life. "Okay, so, if you don't do hospitals, do you bleed to death in alleys? 'Cause if that's what you're going for, you're well on your way, dude." She gave him a thumbs-up. "Way to go."

His gaze moved over her and he shook his head. He shrugged out of his coat and tossed it to her, grimacing.

"Put it on," he said. "I can't even hear myself think over the sound of your teeth chattering."

"Gee, and they say chivalry is dead," she intoned dryly, shoving her arms into the sleeves of the black trench.

The coat was too long by nearly a foot, and the sleeves hung down well below her hands, but the fabric still held the warmth of his skin, and she was far too cold to be concerned with fit or fashion. The *What Not to Wear* folks could just kiss her warm, toasty ass.

He watched her fidget for a while before asking, "Who *are* you?"

"I'm Harper." She shook the sleeves of the coat back, finally finding her hand and extending it to him. "Harper Hall."

He stared at her hand, then raised his gaze to hers. "That explains a lot."

Harper let her hand sink back into the coat's depths and narrowed her eyes on him. "What's that supposed to mean?"

"You were Romeo Jones' seer. That explains why you were willing to take off, alone, after a vamp three-times your size with a chair leg." His gaze moved over her again, slowly. "In your underwear."

She put her hand on her hip and cocked her head to one side. "Are you insulting me, or are you insulting Romeo? Because if you're insulting me, you and I need to have a serious come-to-Jesus meeting."

For a split second, he looked like he might smile, but just when she was deciding whether to go after him with her make-shift stake or chick-fight him with her fingernails, the smile died and pain flashed through his eyes.

"Let's just say your reputation precedes you," he said, hunching over almost imperceptibly.

Hmmpphh. Noah Riddick talking trash about her reputation. Wasn't that just rich beyond belief?

"Well, hello there, Pot, they call me Kettle," she said dryly. "I hear you're black."

He raised one eyebrow and took a step toward her, only to sway drunkenly before falling to his knees. "Fuck," he muttered, one hand on the ground, one hand on his stomach.

Harper rushed to his side, but he stopped her with a fierce scowl. "I'm not Romeo," he hissed. "I don't need your help."

She straightened and planted her hands on her hips again.

"Look, I've taken about all the shit I intend to from you. So, as I see it, you've got two choices: you can lay there and bleed to death, or you can suck up your stupid male pride and let me help you."

He looked at her like he'd rather rip his heart out with his bare hands than accept her help, but after what must have been an exhausting battle of pride and necessity, he allowed her to ease her shoulder under his arm and help him stand.

Leaning heavily on her, he whispered, "No hospitals," right before he passed out.

Harper staggered under his weight, but somehow managed to keep them both vertical. After a moment of struggling and cussing, she was able to lean him against the dumpster and hold him upright with her bodyweight while she mulled her options.

He didn't want to go to the hospital, and probably rightfully so.

If there were any pro-vamp zealots out there looking for a little slayer-bashing action, he'd be a sitting duck in the hospital.

She couldn't take him back into the Kitty Kat Palace. Bleeding men tended to draw attention there as well.

That really only left one viable option.

Boy, if Riddick thought she was reckless now, wait until he woke up in her bed.

Like it so far? All books in the Harper Hall Investigations series are now available from all major book sellers. Happy reading!

The Harper Hall Investigations series reading order (all books now available everywhere books are sold):

Book 1: Semi-Charmed

Book 2: Semi-Human

Book 3: Semi-Twisted

Book 4: Semi-Broken

Book 5: Semi-Sane

Book 5.5: Semi-Obsessed

ABOUT THE AUTHOR

The normal:

Isabel Jordan writes because it's the only profession that allows her to express her natural sarcasm and not be fired. She is a paranormal and contemporary romance author. Isabel lives in the U.S. with her husband, 12-year-old son, a neurotic shepherd mix, and a ginormous Great Dane mix named Jerkface (but don't feel bad for him. He's earned the name).

The weird:

Now that the normal stuff is out of the way, here's some weird-but-true facts that would never come up in polite conversation. Isabel Jordan:

1. Is terrified of butterflies (don't judge ... it's a real phobia called lepidopterophobia)

2. Is a lover of all things ironic (hence the butterfly on the original cover of *Semi-Charmed*)

3. Is obsessed with *Supernatural, Game of Thrones, The Walking Dead, The* 100, *Once Upon a Time*, and *Dog Whisperer*.

4. Hates coffee. Drinks a Diet Mountain Dew every morning.

5. Will argue to the death that *Pretty in Pink* ended all wrong. (Seriously, she ends up with the guy who was embarrassed to be seen with her and not the nice guy who loved her all along? That would never fly in the world of romance novels.)

6. Would eat Mexican food every day if given the choice.

7. Reads two books a week in varied genres.

8. Refers to her Kindle as "the precious."

9. Thinks puppy breath is one of the best smells in the world.

10. Is a social media idgit. (Her husband had to explain to her what the point of Twitter was. She's still a little fuzzy on what Instagram and Pinterest do.)

11. Kicks ass at Six Degrees of Kevin Bacon.

12. Stole her tagline idea ("weird and proud") from her son. Her tagline idea was, "Never wrong, not quite right." She liked her son's idea better.

13. Breaks one vacuum cleaner a year because she ignores standard maintenance procedures (Really, you're supposed to empty the canister every time you vacuum? Does that seem excessive to anyone else?)

14. Is still mad at the WB network for cancelling *Angel* in 2004.

15. Can't find her way from her bed to her bathroom without her glasses, but refused eye surgery, even when someone else offered to pay. (They lost her at "eye flap". Seriously, look it up. Scary stuff.)

Made in the USA
Middletown, DE
29 August 2020